Blood That Speaks

Roseann Gilbody

PublishAmerica
Baltimore

ISBN: 1-60563-518-9
PUBLISHED BY PUBLISHAMERICA, LLLP
www.publishamerica.com
Baltimore

Printed in the United States of America

For Kathleen, Laure, Roseann and Rick
who helped me take that next step

Blood
That Speaks

Chapter 1

Rita would have ignored her Aunt Louisa-Maria's urgent request to come to Boston but she felt she owed the old woman. Her Aunt had taken over her care when her parents were killed in a boating accident when Rita was ten years old. Louisa-Maria had made sure Rita kept up her appointments with Dr. Sherry. She had held her small hand firmly, just like her Father had. Every other week He had sat on that dark blue sofa in that overdone French Antique waiting room. Rita clearly remembered how awkward he always looked with his long legs, knees askew, tight fists hanging between, head bent. She thought he must have been the only man to ever wait in Dr. Sherry's ugly waiting room. And every time she came back out he would look up with that tiny flame of hope in his eyes. Quickly extinguished by the litany of lies poured out of Dr. Sherry's thin red lips "some progress, slow, but much better, I do see a tiny improvement." Her father would look down at her and take her small hand in his and they would leave the overdone waiting room. How she loved those weeks. She always listened carefully to her Father's voice but she could never bring up any words to join in his quiet, funny conversations.

She remembered fondly how Louisa-Maria had been disgusted at the lack of progress in her recovery and quickly fired Dr. Sherry and hired young Dr. Timothy Byrd. Thank God. Louisa was definitely a really smart old woman. She nibbled the cube of cheese and stared down at the lights of Little Italy in Boston's famous North End.

"Boston beans. Boston beans," squawked the big grey bird in the ornate cage

"It's 'baked beans' T-Bird. Boston Baked Beans. Say it right if you are going to say it." Rita grinned and fed the parrot a piece of cheese from the tray set out on the sidetable. "Yummy, T-Bird. Your favorite. Provolone." The small piece of cheese was lifted gently out of Rita's fingers by a shiny black beak Rita turned her gaze back to the bright night lights shining outside the windows.

Staring out the massive floor to ceiling window, Rita's trained artist eye studied the opposite building still under construction. It was such a contrast to the smaller red brick buildings down in the shadows. Rita could almost smell the wonderful, aromas that always wafted out to the cobblestone sidewalks. Such fun to walk along and peek into all the small family restaurants. She fondly remembered the small corner restaurant on Hanover and Beall. Tony Rizzo's.

After her appointment with Dr. Sherry and they would always have the same lunch. Escarole soup and antipasto salad. Lots of delicious pickings in the salad. Little squares of different cheeses, thin slices of salami and some kind of ham, lots of black olives. She would take a long time eating each separate morsel. Loving the sound of her father's voice as he chatted in Italian with the many friends that would always be at Tony's. But now so far down She wondered sadly if she would ever again feel that warmth.

"Provolone. Cheese, Cheese. My favorite. Favorite," called out the big grey parrot. Rita turned from the window "This is it' T-Bird. No more cheese today." Just then Louisa-Maria swept into the room. Elegant as always in a floor length pale ivory robe.

"Oh, my dear Rita," Louisa hugged and kissed Rita soundly on both cheeks. "Must you bring that noisy creature everytime?" Louisa glared at T-Bird.

"Louisa-Maria. Louisa-Maria. Pretty name. Pretty name," the big grey sprang up to his swing, swaying gently his sharp eyes on Louisa. "Can't stand the old bird. Noisy old bird."

"My stars, what a creature! Well do help yourself." Louisa already was sipping on a small glass of Amaretto. So Rita quickly poured a glass of Merlot smothering a little grin. They sat on the long white sofa facing the panoramic view of the Boston skyline.

"So Louisa, what is the big mystery? What is going on? And why couldn't you tell me on the phone? Also, why the lawyers?"

One thin veined hand waved at Rita while the other lifted the crystal glass to her dry lips. "Numero uno, my dear, you are one of the last remaining Bondones, the end of the bloodline of an old respectable Urbino family and..."

"Aren't you forgetting Paul?" Rita interrupted.

"That monster, that weak alcoholic bastard. A curse on his flaming head," the old woman slammed the crystal glass onto the marble coffee table shattering the fragile stem of the delicate glass.

"Oh, Louisa," Rita gasped leaping up to relieve the shaking old woman of the broken glass and brush the pieces of the shattered stem into the large ash tray on the table.

"Oh, never mind that. Just get me another Amaretto," she said harshly.

"I'm so sorry, Loiusa-Maria. I didn't mean to upset you," Rita saw her Aunt's blue eyes brimming with unshed tears. The old woman stroked Rita's short, blonde curls.

"Ahh, my child life is hard and much too short. Come now I forgive you. We must talk tomorrow. Dry your eyes," the bony hand pressed a lacy handkerchief to her niece's tear-stained face. "You must fly to Urbino the day after tomorrow."

This announcement uttered so flatly, sent Rita reeling back on her heels. She stared at Louisa-Maria open mouthed.

"Do shut your mouth, dear. You look hideous," Louisa stood up and walked majestically to her bedroom door. "I shall expect you for breakfast at eight. The lawyers will be here so be prompt." The cream colored door shut quietly on the ivory clad figure. And

Rita sat on her heels on the lush carpeting twenty stories above Boston, drying her eyes on a scented lace hankie wondering what on earth was going on? Why must I fly to Italy? Especially to Urbino. No. No. I won't go. Rita thought of the shimmering sun-lit roofs hanging precariously on the steep mountainside and a sense of foreboding filled her as she dragged herself to her feet. Shivering she dragged herself to her bedroom and crawled into the huge warm bed. Warm and snug she fell into an exhausted sleep only to dream of strange towers with spiraling staircases, dancing red geraniums and a cold marble tomb.

Chapter 2

Landing in Rome, Rita was met by the Italian side of Armstrong, Collingstone & Mattini. Mr. Domimc Mattini was tall, gray-haired and unsmiling. After a cool introduction he escorted Rita to a long gray Mercedes. Mr. Mattini did not seem very happy about Rita's appearance in Italy. On the short ride to the hotel the silence in the plush Mercedes was broken only by Mr. Mattini's staccato statements informing Rita that she would be picked up at her hotel in the morning at ten and driven up to Urbino. If she needed any further help to call him at his Rome office at the number listed on his card which he handed to her. Rita sincerely hoped she would not have any cause to call the stiff cold attorney.

Later, in her hotel room Rita ordered a light supper of Fettucinne, tossed salad and a glass of wine. After picking at the food half-heartedly she finally pushed it away and picked up her sketchbook and began outlining the hustle and bustle of Rome's busy streets. Scenes that she had unconsciously absorbed on the short ride from the airport to the hotel. The scene she was now creating was fluid and dynamic stressing the human action and drama of everyday activities. She felt less lonely sitting there in the semi-dark studying her sketchbook. Glancing up she was awed by the beautiful sight outside the open balcony door. The bright lights of the Castel Sant' Angelo flickered over the dark waters of the Tiber river. Built by the brilliant emperor Hadrian in 135 A.D., the sight of the towering castle glowing in the dark night awakened long buried emotions in Rita. Conflicting emotions for she knew Italy was a warm, friendly country yet she was plagued by some strange unknown fear. She had not wanted to return to Urbino but here she was standing on a hotel balcony in the middle of Rome, shivering at the sight of the indestructible ramparts of Castel Sant'Angelo. Turning back into the room she shut and locked the balcony doors pulling the heavy drapes closed. She paced the darkened room too keyed up to draw anymore and too tense to sleep. Staring at Dominic Mattini's small engraved white card Rita wondered why selling an old Villa high in the remote hillside of Urbino would bother him. Just then the shrill ring of the telephone jarred her from her troubled thoughts. She hesitantly lifted the receiver wondering who could be calling her in Rome.

"Signorina Bondone?" a deep voice asked.

"Yes," Rita replied cautiously.

"Signorina, go back to America. Do not go to Urbino. It is dangerous."

"Who is this?" she juggled the phone as the line went dead.

"Hello. Hello." damn. She slammed the phone down. Why would Urbino be dangerous for her? She hadn't been back there since her parents died. She felt tears coming as the memories of the last happy summer with her parents flooded back. She threw herself on the bed, angry and very frightened. Was this some silly prank? Someone who wanted the Villa. Hell, she would sell it to them in a minute. Was there really some kind of danger ahead for her? She was determined not to panic. Forcing herself to stop crying she tried to concentrate her thoughts on that wonderful summer in Urbino when all the Bondones were together at the Villa Sera. Happiness and gaiety filled her life then. She drifted off to sleep remembering those long lost happy days.

But soon her nightmare returned even stronger. Red flowers danced in the air. Bright red blood pooled across pale blue mosaic tiles. Several paintings floated in the air their heavy ornate frame seeming like doorways. She was vainly trying to catch one to enter but they swirled away in the misty air. When she looked down she saw the bright red blood trickling over her white sandals. Ahead off toward the garden fountain two black clad figures sat on a stone bench, heads bent in conversation. Dreamily she floated towards them wishing they would look up. She needed to see their faces. Why didn't they look up? Didn't they know she was there? Suddenly something moved in the fountain. One of the marble statues was stepping out of the fountain basin. A sweet young boy holding a tortoise. His smooth marble skin gleaming whitely amidst the dancing red flowers whirling in the misty air. He now blocked her path and whispered, "Do not go. Do not go." over and over again. Rita flailed at him with her weightless arms.

Struggling amidst the tangled bed cover she woke in a cold sweat. Her heart pounding and trembling with fear. Dragging herself into the bathroom she turned on the hot water and stood under the soothing stream until she calmed down. Toweling off she saw her reflection in the mirror. She stared at the dark circles under her tired blue eyes.

"I look a wreck! One more night of these crazy dreams and I'll look like Louisa-Maria's twin. Which might not be so bad. After all she is eighty and has lived to a ripe old age in spite of the Bondone curse." She hurriedly finished dressing still wondering if there really was a Bondone curse and who was trying to warn her. Warn her of what? What danger lie waiting for her in Urbino?

Exiting the elevator into the busy Lobby her mind a mass of confused thoughts, she had a impulse to call David Swan. They had started to get serious in their relationship and Rita hoped it was finally time for her to find some happiness again. After several minutes, several operators she reached David in his Hartford, Connecticut insurance office. After he had recovered from the shock of her being in Rome, he insisted he take his three weeks vacation time and fly out to her. Happily she hung up the phone, a huge smile spreading across her face. "How wonderful.

David will be here in two days." She beamed turning quickly she was surprised at the very tall, muscular dark-haired man standing right behind her.

"Miss Bond? I'm Carlo Molza. Here let me take that," he plucked her small overnight bag from her hand and without another word marched out of the Hotel. Rita ran after him, her happiness over David's coming quickly replaced by anger at yet another cool, brusque Italian man.

"Well, that's just great," she fumed, "So much for the warm, friendly Italians. Just my luck to meet two of the nastiest." The big man was holding the car door opened for her, the rest of her luggage already tucked into the small rear seat. His dark eyes took in her figure as she hurried over to the red Maserati. She blushed as she caught him staring directly at her breasts which moved heavily as she hurried in her high heels.

"Mr. Molza, what is the big hurry?" she glared at him.

"Siguorina, it's a long drive and I have much to do today. Please get in." He motioned impatiently with his big hand. Then slammed the door sharply after she slipped into the small car. Rita sensed he disapproved of her for some reason. The Maserati responded easily to Carlo's touch, pulling smoothly out into Rome's incredible traffic. They crawled slowly down the Via dei Fori Imperiali towards the Coliseum. The large stadium once covered with marble now quaked under the onslaught of the heavy traffic swirling around it. Rita turned to get a glimpse of the beautiful Arch of Constantine next to the Coliseum. She loved the intricately carved Arch not only for its beauty but also for what it stood for—the end of the persecution of the Christians. Brought about by Constantine's conversion to Christianity after experiencing a vision on the battlefield. The Arch had always made Rita feel happy. As a small child she loved the story of the beautiful Arch. She had never cared to enter the Coliseum with its long history of bloody events.

Her attention was drawn to a laughing young couple in an old Fiat that had pulled up alongside the sleek Maserati. The young man stared enviously at the red sports car but the beautiful young woman quickly distracted him with a brazen kiss on the lips.

"Rome," Rita thought "the Eternal City. City of Hope and Love. Would she someday be able to kiss a man so impetuously?" She stole a glance at the handsome dark-haired stranger beside her. He seemed strangely familiar. Those dark, piercing eyes looked right inside her.

"I'm sorry if I caused you any inconvenience. I could have rented a car and driven myself," she spoke shyly. The dark head turned slightly and with a curt nod and a quick glance accepted her apology.

"I'm sure you could have but I promised Louisa-Maria," his voice was deep and melodious.

"Louisa-Maria? You know my Aunt?" Rita had erroneously assumed he was someone that Dominic Mattini had hired to drive her up to Urbino.

"I know all the Bondones," he stated flatly giving her a long strange look.

Rita looked closer at the tall, serious man. She studied his hard profile. He was extremely handsome in a rough looking way. Muscles flexed and tensed on his long tanned arms as he expertly maneuvered the small car around the hair-pin curves.

His jet black hair framed his tanned face with thick black eyebrows above his piercing dark eyes. His jaw was wide with strong square bones and fleshy well shaped lips were tightly compressed. She could feel the irrepressible energy emanating from the big man. Such energy could overpower her if she wasn't careful. She suddenly felt terribly threatened by this silent dark stranger.

"Well tell me how do you know all the Bondones? I don't remember ever meeting you!" she asked him coolly. His detached, superior attitude was beginning to irritate her already tense nerves.

"Really?" he snapped as he increased their speed. Roaring up and around the sharp curves of the narrow mountain road. Rita glanced nervously to her right. The landscape fell miles straight down. Far below the rooftops poked through the green leafy blanket of trees. Here and there a patch of road winding through quiet pastoral scenes that they had just whizzed by only a scant few minutes ago could be seen.

"Aren't you going rather fast?" she questioned him as she clutched the door handle. She was not going to be thrown any closer to the dark muscular young man if she could avoid it. He gave her a quick, mocking look. Not even bothering to answer, he swept the small red car quickly around a completely blind curve, swaying even more dangerously over to the left. Then swerving easily back over to the right. Pebbles and dirt loosened by the wheels cascaded down the steep incline. Rita let out a tiny gasp and clutched the door handle even tighter while cursing him under her breath. She gritted her teeth, "Damn him. He is deliberately trying to frighten me." She dragged her eyes away from the steep drop-off perilously close to the wheels of the small car and studied the handsome dark stranger once more. His muscular thighs strained as he deftly worked the gas and brake pedals with his scruffy sneakers.

"What are you gawking at?" he growled in his husky voice.

"Just your Adidas. I have a pair also," she snapped back. She was determined to appear unafraid. She quickly averted her gaze back to the road. "What an insufferable macho bore," she thought.

They rode in strained silence. Carlo had swung off the Autostrada onto Route E7 and now were winding through the low green hills and quiet valleys of the landlocked region of Italy known as the Umbria region. They had past through many medieval cities nestled on the sides of the steep hills. Each one seeming more and more to have blended into the natural landscape acquiring a quiet natural dignity. The orange and rose-colored brick buildings had changed little in hundreds of years.

Rita was thrilled to be driving through the very landscapes made so well known by the paintings of Raphael. After several comments about the beauty of the hilly countryside she soon ceased trying to make any conversation with the taciturn, tight-lipped Carlo.

They lost quite a bit of time passing through the large city of Perugia. Spring fever had hit the many students attending the Italian University and the Universita per Stranieri (University for Foreigners). Large crowds of students marched along the narrow streets, arms locked or waving banners. They filled the steps of the Gothic Cathedral with several playing guitars while others sang or smoked or just conversed in small groups. On one particular steep street the small Maserati was brought to a complete halt by a sea of exuberant students. Two attractive young students leaned into the stalled car and flirted outrageously with Carlo. Rita was surprised when the stoical Carlo returned their compliments adding, Rita felt sure by the way the girls laughed and threw back their shoulders, a few ribald comments about their tight T-shirts. She bristled when one of the girls leaned back down to give Carlo a brief kiss before waving and marching on down the steep hill.

"Well while we are stuck here we might as well get some candy," he leaped out and entered a small shop. Returning in several minutes with three large boxes of chocolates which he placed in the back seat on top of her luggage. Settling his long frame once again behind the wheel he drew a small white bag from his pocket.

"Have one. The Perugia chocolate is world famous. You'll never taste one any better," he plopped a candy in his mouth while holding the bag out towards her.

She reached into the white paper bag, her fingers brushing against Carlo's sending a jolt of electricity up her arm. The chocolates were delicious and Rita realized now what the tantalizing aroma was that had been teasing her for the last half-hour. Perugia's famous chocolate factory. She bit hungrily into another of the creamy chocolates. Looking up she found Carlo watching her. Their eyes locked momentarily and Rita felt pure physical desire wash over her. She was sure she saw a gleam of satisfaction in Carlo's dark eyes before he turned to start the engine. A faint smile played on his sensual lips. Rita felt her face burning with shame. She turned and watched the last of the students marching by.

Soon the road became even narrower, winding and twisting as they left Perugia behind and climbed along Route 298 high into the Apennines mountains. Passing Mount Urbino the landscape became dotted with thick forests. The air much cooler. Rita reached in the back seat for her sweater and they drove for several hours before Carlo swung off onto a dirt road which led though a vine covered arch which opened onto a cobblestone piazza. Carlo stopped the car neatly in front of a small trattoria.

"We'll lunch here, Signorina. Come. I'm starved." He

unfolded his long muscular legs out of the little car and then bent to look in at Rita who sat still clutching her sweater.

"Aren't you hungry?" he inquired in a slightly gentler tone.

"Yes, of course," Rita replied snapping open the car door and following Carlo into the trattoria. The owner rushed forward greeting Carlo warmly. It was quickly apparent to Rita that Carlo was well known and respected at the small family owned restaurant. They were promptly seated in the garden courtyard which had a magnificent view of the valley and part of the winding, narrow road they had traveled only moments ago.

A little girl of about seven years old, shyly placed a basket of fresh blue and white wild flowers on their table. She blushed and giggled when Carlo spoke to her in Italian. Rita found she enjoyed the sound of Carlo's deep melodious voice as he entertained the little girl making her laugh gaily until her father returned to send her back to the kitchen. Carlo's dark eyes sparkled warmly and Rita suddenly wished that for a brief moment he might look at her in such a manner. But the tenderness vanished from his eyes when he turned back to face her. She felt a strange sense of loss sweep over her. She needed someone. She didn't want to be alone with this dark, handsome stranger. His very nearness disturbed her. "Whatever is the matter with me? If only David were here. It's such a beautiful spot. Certainly not the place to be with such a man like Carlo," she thought sadly.

She turned away from the hard, piercing eyes and began studying the road far below them. Maybe he would stop watching her so intently if she ignored him for a while. She saw a tiny black speck weaving its way upward. As she followed its progress upwards she heard the waiter returning with their lunch. Carlo had ordered without even consulting her. She fumed inwardly but quickly resigned herself to Carlo's independent attitude as she was too tired and feeling a little jet-lag from her flight the previous day. Besides being much too hungry having skipped breakfast. The chocolates had only whetted her appetite. The meal being placed before her smelled delicious.

The pavase, a clear chicken broth with bits of egg and escarole floating in it was followed with shrimp scampi, swimming in the excellent butter produced up here in the mountain region. She ate heartily, breaking off pieces of the fresh baked bread to soak up the buttery garlic sauce. She washed it down with several glasses of the tart greenish-white "Verdicchio" wine. She was enjoying the food so much she had dimly been aware of Carlo across the small table. He was finishing a dish of mixed greens when a decidedly agitated young man hurried to their table. He whispered in Carlo's ear while casting quick glances at Rita. They both looked past Rita down towards the winding road. She could see that the tiny black speck was now a long black car weaving smoothly up the narrow road.

"Come!" Carlo stood quickly spilling Rita's wine. Grabbing her arm he propelled her to the car. Rita fumed inwardly, licking the sticky wine from her fingers. She snapped angrily at him, "Well, I would have liked to finish my wine!" His dark eyes followed her tongue licking and sucking her sticky fingers. Their eyes locked and Rita felt the heat from his hard eyes penetrating her whole body. Quickly she dropped her hand. Again she was embarrassed at the raw sensuality she saw in Carlo's handsome face. She lowered her eyes wiping her fingers hurriedly on her skirt. She was relieved when he finally spoke breaking the spell of togetherness that had sprung between them in the small cramped car.

"I'll make sure we share another bottle of wine later in Urbino he drawled huskily, pulling the sleek little sports car quickly onto the narrow road. Rita sat deeply shaken. Never had she felt so physically drawn towards any man. She stole a glance at Carlo. He was driving very fast again, concentrating intently on the many curves which seemed to come at them every few minutes. Up and up the small car raced. Several times she fell against Carlo's broad shoulder as they roared around the sharp turns. Their bare arms brushing and sending electric feelings ricocheting through her tense body. Rita pulled herself way over to the right. Grasping the door handle her head felt woozy, her body flushed. "It must be the wine," she thought. She wanted nothing further to do with her angry, virile driver.

Carlo was casting anxious looks in the rear-view mirror. The long, black car was coming up close behind them. Now it seemed very ominous as the windows were all dark glass. The big black car crowded the small Maserati on the narrow road. Pressing on the gas Carlo quickly pulled away from the other car. His face hardened, his jaw thrust forward. Animal power coiled in his tall frame. Rita squirmed uneasily in her seat she detected a new smell mixing with their garlicky breath. The big car was gaining, little by little it ate up the distance separating the two cars. She cast a frightened glance out her window. The edge of the road was only inches away. "So far, far down," she thought terrified. Suddenly a scream flew from her tight throat as the big car nudged the small Maserati towards the edge of the road. But Carlo held fast pulling hard to the left. Rita prayed that no car would appear coming around the bend or they would be killed head-on. Suddenly she realized what the strange scent was in the small cramped car. Fear. The smell of fear—of death. This was a duel to the death. Below her far down the mountainside fields of red flowers swayed in the soft afternoon breeze. She turned back to Carlo as she felt him braking slightly slowing their pace and allowing the big car to gain on them. "Good Lord what is he doing," she thought frantically. Then metal clanged against metal as the big car pushed against the smaller car trying to thrust it over the edge. Rita was frantic as earth and stones flew down the mountain side as the right side of the Maserati hung suspended over empty space. The fields of red flowers swayed before Rita's terrified eyes. "The dancing flowers of my dream," she thought as the scent of impending death permeated her every fiber and just when she was surrendering herself to certain death. Carlo threw his large body against the steering wheel dragging them from certain death. The lighter Maserati pulled quickly to the far left while the heavier black car plowed like an angry bull off the road and down the steep incline, tumbling over and over until it burst into bright red flames among the soft green olive trees.

It was several minutes before Rita regained her senses. She had been thrown violently over to the left of the small car where the steering wheel dug painfully into her ribs. Carlo's strong arms drew her gently into his broad chest. She didn't want to open her terrified eyes. She wanted to stay as close to his strong warm body as possible. She felt his hard chest muscles pressing against her trembling breast. She felt his racing heart beating beneath his sweat soaked shirt. She nuzzled her face into his warm pulsing neck. A strong hand pulled her head up and hot demanding lips pressed fiercely on her soft trembling lips. A red hot tongue savagely explored her mouth. The spices of their lunch adding titillating flames to the burning kiss. Carlo's mouth was a seething volcano ready to devour her. Demanding what she couldn't give. Not yet. Her heart cried out to him "there's been so much Death" she pleaded silently with him while her lips told him differently. Carlo's big hand ran down her side pressing hard on her hip. Drawing her thighs towards him. He whispered frantic, hoarse phrases in her ear. Although she couldn't understand the Italian words she felt their sensual meanings. Rita froze, drawing away from him.

"What did you say?" she demanded as Carlo repeated the amorous Italian phrases, drawing her back and kissing her neck.

"No, I mean what did you just call me?" she tried vainly to pull back but Carlo hugged her even closer.

"I called you 'Margarita,' mi amore," he kissed her neck again.

"No, no," Rita pushed violently at Carlo's big chest.

"What's wrong?" he asked surprised at her sudden change. She moved stiffly to the other side of the car.

"My name is Rita Bond. Why did you call me Magarita?" she glared at him.

"Because that is your name. Margarita Bondone. And why did you change it anyway?" he toyed with her golden hair, his powerful arm resting on the back of the seat. Angrily she pushed his hand away.

"Please," she pleaded. "I'm scared and tired. Can't we go? We should notify the police," she suddenly found that she did not want to explain her tragic life to this strange, bold man who had just saved her from certain death. He had such a quiet confidence and a very mysterious familiarity that unsettled her. No, she didn't want to be so close to him. She moved away straightening her skirt which had risen up over her knees. Carlo stared long and hard at her anxious face. He was confused by Rita's sudden change of mood. He studied her bruised face. His dark eyes filling with concern and desire. Rita felt herself weakening. She realized she wanted him to hold her, to feel his warm lips again but something inside her held her back. She really did not want to be drawn back to this rugged mountain country. There were too many dark shadows. Too much sadness. She silently cursed her

Aunt Louisa-Maria for dragging her back to Urbino. Back to the past. She tore her eyes from Carlo, afraid that he could see her doubts and fears mirrored in her eyes.

"Margarita…"

"No please!" she wrung her trembling hands together, "Let's just go." Carlo started the engine with a deep sigh and they finished the journey to Urbino in chilly silence.

Rounding a sharp curve Rita gasped, not so much at Carlo's fast driving but more for the bright jewel of a city that spread out before her eyes. She had forgotten the beauty of Urbino. The lovely city wound its way between two imposing mountains. Avenues, streets and homes climbing and winding their way up the side of the left mountain. In the valley nestled the large municipal buildings. The big white Government House, the many scattered buildings of the City University and the blunt rose colored square edifice housing the Historical Society. Next to that the sparkling white marble Opera House. Rita was amazed that she could still identify these buildings as Carlo whizzed through the town with the occasional toot of the horn and a hearty wave to smiling townsfolk. It was many years since she had been back to Urbino. The city had grown. Spreading out in all directions. New streets cut off to the right leading to beautiful new villas built precariously on the side of the mountain. Here and there she could still see old roads of cobblestone climbing zigzag up the mountain. These older streets were crowded with pushcarts. Vendors selling fresh green and yellow vegetables. Carts loaded with every color of fragrant flower imaginable, mixed with the smell of hot spicy sausages sizzling on glowing charcoal braziers all blending with the butchered smell of fresh chicken, rabbits and lamb all hanging pale and lifeless, swaying on a wobbly crooked cart while its owner bellowed his ware's virtues to the high third floor windows along the crowded street. Little children laughing and screaming chased barking dogs in and out amongst the carts causing even more noise and confusion. The city's main street was crowded with delivery trucks, the main life-line of this high mountain region and Carlo was forced to reduce his speed.

A tiny smile touched the corner's of Rita's pink lips. All the noise, the colors the people bustling about…here was life. She felt a surge of joy through her whole body. She was so happy to be alive. She looked over at Carlo. Their eyes met and he gave her a brief happy grin. She smiled gratefully back. She didn't understand why the big Alfretta attempted to push them off the road. But she knew in her heart if she had been driving alone she would now be dead at the bottom of that ravine. She clasped her arms hugging herself tightly. As they passed the impressive Church of San Giovanni she silently said a prayer of thanks for her life and the handsome man beside her.

Chapter 3

Leaving the city of Urbino behind the small car climbed even higher up the soaring mountain until they finally turned into a drive blocked by massive ornate iron gates. With a quick wave to the guards they passed through and soon were at the main door of Villa San Giovanni.

Later in her spacious sunny room Rita lay on the big bed with a cool cloth over her aching eyes. She was relieved that her reception at the Villa had been warm and friendly. The Barlettas, the old couple that oversaw the large Villa had been shocked when they heard about the harrowing ride up from Rome. Aldo Barletta had immediately placed a call to the Urbino Polizia and was assured they would send a man to the Villa after the Signorina had a chance to rest. Sofia had brought some aspirins and the cool compress for the black and blue lump that was beginning to swell on her forehead.

"Poor Signorina, what a terrible welcome to Urbino. I'll call Father Vincenzo. His blessing will chase away those evil spirits plaguing you. Poor dear," she fussed and bustled about unpacking Rita's bags. Fuming about the beauty and serenity of Urbino being ruined by evil elements from the South. She reminisced about the old days when her own mother looked after the Villa.

"How long have you been here Sofia?" Rita asked.

"Aha, how long. Always. I was born right here. Like most of the folks in Urbino my family goes back many centuries," and with that she closed the door gently finally leaving Rita in blessed quiet.

The dreams came while she dozed fitfully. Only this time there were no dancing red flowers. Just the fountain and the bench off to the side where the two hooded figures sat huddled conspiritally together. The statue of the young-faun again blocked her path. He held something out to her. The gray mist swirled around her concealing the object. Then Carlo's face was floating towards her. The dark eyes sad, the sensual lips pleading, "Margarita, Margarita." Rita woke with a start. She could still hear the husky voice calling her name. She sat up, pulling her knees up she rested her chin in her hands. For several minutes she pondered this new mystery. No one outside of her Aunt Louisa-Maria and her cousin Paul knew her real name. She had refused to use it after her namesake, Aunt Margarita, took her own life by jumping off the Mystic River Bridge. The shame of her only son turning out an alcoholic just like her husband, the unforgivable pain and sorrow he had caused to those who had tried to help him. The tragedy of the fire. These were all burdens too heavy for the petite Margarita O'Neil. Her bloated body was recovered three days after her purse and farewell note were found on the upper level of the tall bridge. Rita never wanted to hear that name again. To her it meant weakness and shame.

Furiously, she brushed away the tears. How could Carlo know her real name? Certainly Louisa would never tell anyone. She respected Rita's feelings only too well and rarely spoke her dead sister's name herself. So it had to be Paul. But how could Carlo know Paul O'Neil? Rita turned these thoughts over and over while she soaked in the beautiful marble tub. Hearing the outer door to her room open, she stepped from the tub, slipping into a short blue silk robe. She called out, "Sofia, has my cousin" she stopped short. Not Sofia but Carlo stood in the middle of the bedroom. Surprised, she pulled her thin robe together wishing it was a heavy terry-cloth. Carlo's dark eyes told her what she was acutely aware of. . . that her thin silk robe was hardly covering her nudity.

"What do you want? How dare you barge in here!" Rita stood still afraid to move and show anymore of her nude body beneath the silky robe.

"I did knock. I was worried when you didn't answer," his wide grin mocking her modesty. He began moving towards her.

"Oh, no. Stay right there!" Rita wished for some heavier cover something to protect her from his hungry eyes. She edged towards the closet and in doing so the flimsy silk robe gaped open exposing her right breast. Hurriedly she clutched the robe closed but Carlo in one swift movement was directly in front of her. She could feel his warm breath on her nervous lips. She looked defiantly into his dark eyes.

"Get out," she snapped at him. Afraid of him and her own strong physical attraction to the tall stranger. She hugged her folded arms across her chest.

"Don't worry Rita. I never have to force my women," he held her lightly by the shoulders drawing her trembling body close to his broad chest. He kissed her gently on her bruised forehead. His warm soft lips brushed across her eyelids before finding her own slightly parted lips. A kiss so gentle yet firm and insistent sent waves of desire rushing though Rita's tense body. She felt an overwhelming need to lose herself in these strong arms. She had never reacted either mentally or physically to any man as she now was responding to Carlo Molza. The depth of her desire frightened her. She pushed him away averting her head to avoid his dark hypnotic eyes. Once more she told him, "Please leave. Your rude advances really are not welcome."

"Don't be silly. You are not a child. You've enjoyed both of the kisses I have given you. Just relax sweetheart it can be wonderful," his hands caressed her back sliding down over her round buttocks. Pressing her body tightly against his own. He kissed her neck and she felt his dark hair tickling her chin.

She smelled his after-shave something aromatic and very

masculine. She knew she had to get away from him before she lost all control. Once again she pushed hard on his big chest. Her eyes were blazing at him, "Get out. I don't want you here...you whoever you are."

He looked hurt for a brief moment then his eyes clouded over. He stared coldly at her before stepping back and releasing her. "You don't know what you want, Margarita." He strode to the door, turning he spoke softly, "Next time you'll come to me."

Furious Rita picked up a sneaker and flung it at the closing door. "Bastard!" she screamed. Her thoughts whirled around in her throbbing head. She kept remembering how he had held her in the small car after the accident. His kiss, his strong arms had promised her safety and security. But now she felt so threatened by his kisses, his virile caresses. The more she thought about Carlo the more confused and upset she became. "I must stop thinking about him in that way. I must find out who he is and how he knows my real name. And how does he know ALL the Bondones. Thank heavens David will be here the day after tomorrow. She felt better thinking of quiet, calm David.

Chapter 4

Approaching the candlelit dining room, hearing soft feminine laughter followed by a low provocative male voice Rita felt her back stiffen. Her own feminine instincts raced wildly. She was very surprised to see so many people seated around the long beautiful old diinng table. She thought it would be only the Barlettas, Carlo and herself. Where had all these people come from? She experienced a brief flicker of disappointment at not being alone with Carlo but it was quickly dispelled by her astonishment at the sight of her Aunt Louisa-Maria resplendent in a pale mauve gown. The old woman sat regally at the head of the long table. Several of the men rose as she entered and the woman in the mauve dress spoke rapidly in Italian and they quickly sat, bowing and smiling at Rita.

"Ah, my darling American. Welcome to Urbino," she reached for Rita planting two dry kisses on each blushing cheek. "You look quite rested from your harrowing ride from Rome. Carlo has told us all about it. Come, dear, sit here," she gestured to an empty chair on her left. Rita slumped gratefully into the plush velvet seat. Not sure her knees could hold her another minute. The flickering candles, the sea of strange faces plus the shock of seeing Louisa…only it wasn't Louisa…rattled her already fragile nerves.

Suddenly a strong firm hand grasped her shoulder, Rita turned and found herself staring into Carlo's dark eyes.

"Rita, I see you don't remember your Aunt Andrea sister to Louisa-Maria," he said sarcastically.

"Now, dear, don't fret. It will all come back to you in due time," she patted Rita's hand gently. Carlo softened his tone and went on to introduce the others sitting at the table. He carefully explained the family ties at each introduction all the while watching Rita's face to make sure she clearly understood. It seemed very important to him that she did. Rita felt tremendously grateful to him for his kindness Her trembling slowly subsided as the warm, firm hand kneaded her tight shoulder. The strong, low voice gave names and quick histories to the strange faces. Rita was amazed to hear her own voice steady and firm acknowledging the introductions. When they were all finished, she turned back to Carlo, his face so close, those warm full lips so inviting. Rita was again amazed at the change in his face now so tender and protective towards her. "Grazie," she whispered, longing to gently kiss the full lips. He gave her shoulder a final squeeze before returning to his seat which Rita unhappily noticed was beside the beautiful young dark-haired woman with the provocative voice. Felicianna that was her name. They made a very striking couple she thought. Her attention was drawn away from the laughing couple by Aunt Andrea's probing question.

"How many months will you live at Villa Sera?"

"Oh, I'm not planning to live at Villa Sera at all," she stared at the old woman wondering why Louisa had never mentioned her sister here in Italy. She was sure she detected a flicker of disappointment in Andrea's hazel eyes. "Louis-Maria told me the Villa hasn't been used in almost fifteen years. It would probably be too expensive to refurbish and besides by life is in Connecticut now." David's thin handsome face and blue eyes coming quickly to mind. Yes, David would help her with all these selling details. He was so level-headed. So cool. She certainly trusted him more than that sour-faced lawyer from Rome. For some reason she felt she needed someone to lean on up here in these rugged mountains. Her confidence in herself had been badly shaken by the near fatal accident. Carlo's quick thinking while she froze in panic weighed on her mind. She needed to be more assertive.

"Louisa-Maria said you were going to spend the summer here," Kay deSica coldly stated, her gold bracelets jingling on her slender wrist as she raised her wine glass to her thin red lips. Her sharp green eyes flashing haughtily back at Rita. The deSicas spent every summer in Urbino preferring the cool mountain air to the humidity of New York city.

"Well, I'm not," Rita answered challenging the green eyes. She was in no mood to explain her reasons to this tall thin aging model. Plus she was furious at Louisa for planning her whole summer behind her back.

"Of course you probably were too young to remember the fine job of remodeling your parents did years ago but I really believe you will find the Villa in fairly livable condition," Greg deSica continued in a soft conciliatory tone. He seemed embarrassed by his wife's brittle attitude. Rita sensed the tall, silver-haired quiet man spent a lot of time smoothing out the sharp waves his attractive wife created.

He smiled hopefully at Rita who returned the gentle man's smile with a brilliant one of her own. "Thank you, Greg. But as I said before my life and career are centered in the States." she thought proudly of her last painting now being shown at the Barnes Gallery and earning some decent reviews.

"Well my dear, you've only just arrived and not in a very pleasant arrival at that. Later we'll talk again about staying longer." Andrea patted her hand again. Then went on to chat gaily about the historical aspects of Urbino. Her love of the area showed through in her stories and Rita became entirely engrossed in the tales of "The Marches" as the region was called. A long ago frontier province of the great empire of Charlemagne. The whole region a German "Mark" of the Charlemagne empire was donated to the Church which in turn had to fight constantly with the great lords from the ruling families. The Sforzas, Malalestas, and the Molzas who for hundreds of years had lived in Urbino.

"Carlo's father is the "grand seigneur." He sent Carlo to be educated in America and now he hardly ever returns," she stated sadly. Rita looked down the long food-laden table where Carlo sat next to the beautiful Felicianna. Her long dark hair cascaded onto her pale shoulders. The low-necked blue dress showing off her full breasts. Carlo and Felicianna were smiling warmly at each other, heads bent in conversation. She lowered her eyes to her plate suddenly uncomfortable in the tight turtleneck she had thrown on earlier. "Sorry Aunt Andrea what did you say?" it had been something about Carlo in the States. Andrea looked closely at Rita, her hazel eyes taking in Rita's discomfit. "Carlo's return from America has pleased his father but not so his elder brother Dante. There has always been a rivalry between them but now 'mio Dio'." She shook her head sadly looking down the table at Carlo.

"That Felicianna she is a temptress, no?" the old woman glanced back at Rita.

"Yes, she certainly is beautiful." Rita answered gazing again at the pale skin and dark flowing hair. She could see how Felicianna managed to keep Carlo in such a warm, sensual mood. She remembered the few fleeting moments of tenderness with Carlo and she realized that she longed for more tender moments with the dark, muscular young man.

"Well, if you are not staying the summer, then what are your plans for Villa Sera?" Kay deSica questioned Rita again. Who stared back at the pencil thin platinum haired model…puzzled by

Kay's obvious animosity, Rita struggled to answer the challenging green eyes. Rita lifted her wineglass forcing herself to maintain eye contact with Kay, while her insides turned over and over. She wondered why one of the world's most photographed models resented an ordinary looking, struggling artist like herself. Surely I'm no threat to her in the looks department for she had noticed the flashing looks Kay had given Carlo and she had felt her heart miss a beat everytime he returned Kay's look with a slight sensual grin and a lascivious glint in his dark eyes.

"I am going to sell the Villa Sera," she answered evenly surprised that her hand shook as she replaced the wineglass on the damask cloth. Silence followed her announcement. All eyes turned to Rita who after a moment of embarrassing awkwardness stubbornly refused to have to justify her actions to the whole table of strangers. Andrea was the first to break the silence "Please, everyone into the Library for coffee and brandy."

Inside the heavily paneled room the large leather fireside couch offered a safe haven for Rita. She sat with Andrea and Father Vincenzo. The husky priest looked more like a wrestler than the soft spoken gentleman he really was. His light humor helped to dispel some of her tenseness and she began to relax. As Father Vincenzo spoke on about the tenacious courage and pride of the mountain folk up here in "The Marches" Rita began to admire the rugged individual people whose lives were filled with tragedies but somehow they managed to go on and not with bitterness but gracefully. She realized she could learn much from these complex noble people.

"You must visit our little church, Signorina. The Church of San Giovanni. Not only is it lovely itself but it gives you a splendid view of the Ducal Palace. I would be happy to escort you on a tour of our town and the Ducal Palace," offered Father Vincenzo with a merry twinkle in his eye.

"Oh, ho you old goat," Andrea playfully nudged the priest with her elbow. "How proud you would be to strut around town with a beautiful blonde Americano. Whatever would people think Vincenzo?" Andrea laughed gaily.

"At my age, Andrea who cares what people think," the two old friends smiled at each other. Father Vincenzo winked happily at Rita, "Anytime you need a friend, Signorina, think of me."

"Thank you, Father. That's the nicest offer I've had since I arrived in Urbino. She had a slight chill thinking of Carlo and his flagrant advances. She sipped the strong clear Sambuco. Relishing the warmth of the liquor, the blazing fire and the new friendships in Father Vincenzo and Andrea. For she had come to realize the old woman really had Rita's best interest at heart. Also she sensed a deep respect between the two older people sitting with her on the couch. Rita felt completely relaxed for the first time since arriving. She had a strange feeling that Louisa was also here in the library sharing this moment with her, Andrea and Father Vincenzo. One big happy family. Strange she thought, shaking her head trying to bring herself back to reality. She looked around the room. It was then she noticed another tall, handsome man had joined them in the Library. He stood just a little shorter than Carlo making him about six-one. The family resemblance was unmistakable. He paused briefly to speak to Carlo and Felicianna, kissing her lightly on her pale cheek. Then he strode quickly over to the fireside couch.

Andrea, mia bellisima," he kissed her soundly and shook hands with Father Vincenzo then turned to Rita, "And the gorgeous Americana. Louisa-Maria's letters did not lie. You are very beautiful," he leaned to kiss her warmly on both cheeks.

"My Aunt wrote you about me?" Rita blurted out completely surprised.

"But of course. My father corresponds regularly with Louisa-Maria." Dante answered smiling charmingly at her. A cold sense of betrayal flooded over Rita. Why had Louisa never mentioned writing to anyone in Urbino? Why had she never even mentioned all these so-called relatives? What on earth was going on? Her nerves tensed up and the cozy camaraderie of the fireside was shattered. "Everyone in this room knows more than I do," she thought desperately. She looked around the library spotting Carlo and Felicianna still chatting by the door, Ernesto and Greg deSica pausing in their game of chess to look up casually as Kay deSica gave Rita a smug smile before returning her attention to the two chess players.

"Good Heavens," Rita thought frantically, "what have I walked into? They are all strangers to me but apparently they all know quite a bit about me. Oh why didn't Louisa warn her? None of these people seem very happy about me being here in Urbino. What could they possible care about the sale of a mountainside Villa that has been closed for over fifteen years?" Her perplexed surveillance of the intimate group gathered in the library was interrupted by the maid Sofia announcing the arrival of the "Polizia."

A short fat man, his bald head gleaming in the firelight, bounced into the library. He was across the room in seconds, his roly-poly looks concealing his quick agility. Bowing slightly to Andrea he kissed the ring clad hand extended towards him.

"Signora Feltre, it is an honor to be of service to you. The Corpo di Vigili Urbani, the city watch, will do all in its power to settle this most unfortunate incident. That a member of such an honored family should be welcomed so harshly to The Marches is unthinkable." The fat little man turned to Rita, bowing and grasping her hand to plant a cool kiss on her fingers.

"Signorina, my deepest apologies for the stupid, dangerous driving of my countrymen. Thank God that Carlo was with you," he gave Carlo a respectful nod. "An expert driver, Signorina…imagine if you alone were driving," he gave a deep sigh.

Rita again experienced the same wave of terror she had as the small Maserarti hung over the side of the mountain. Then the big black Alfretta tumbling down the mountain and bursting into flames among the olive trees. Yes, she thought she could only too well imagine what might have happened had she been driving alone. She sought Carlo's eyes across the room. The dark eyes bore into her hard and cold as if warning her of what she knew not. Dimly she heard the little inspectore speak to her pulling her eyes from Carlo she attempted to answer all the Inspectore's questions. He was quick, precise and very thorough. It was clear he wanted to impress Andrea Feltre. Finally he snapped shut his thin black book bounced lightly to his feet and fairly skipped out of the library.

"Foolishness. Utter foolishness!" snarled Ernesto Feltre, leaving the chess table to confront Andrea, Father Vincenzo and Rita seated before the fireplace. "You know who they were," he insisted to Andrea.

"No I do not, Ernesto. Please be quiet." She waved her hand trying to dismiss him but Ernesto persisted.

"Of course you do. They are from the South. From Napoli. It begins all over again. I told you. I told you. It never ends!" Ernesto wrung his hands shaking his head sadly. He was becoming completely unstrung and Rita sensed the mood changing in the now quiet room.

"Do sit down, Ernesto before you frighten our guest." Andrea admonished him. Father Vincenzo stood, "Come along, Ernesto. There's no need to get upset. Everything will be taken care of. The Inspectore and Carlo have things under control," he led the distressed Ernesto out of the Library.

"Pay no attention to Ernesto, my dear," Andrea turned to Rita. "My brother is always so dramatic."

"But what begins all over again? I must know. You must tell me, Andrea. I can not go on in the dark like this," Rita pleaded. Leaning close to the older woman she saw tears brimming the hazel eyes. "Oh, please. Aunt Andrea. I could have been killed and I don't even know why. You can help me. Tell me about these men."

"Oh, my child. It was so long ago. For centuries these mountains have seen men fighting men. If only Don Fabrizio had never traveled to Napoli. None of this would ever have happened. But he did go. Sent by his family to pick up their many treasures coming in by ship at the Bay of Napoli. But Fate intervened, the ship was late arriving and Don Fabrizio had many nights to dine with the other wealthy ship owners. He fell in love and the curse was born." The tears threatened to flow down her lined cheeks.

"What curse?" Rita dreaded what she must hear. She saw Carlo whirl around and start towards their small group by the fire. But Andrea glared at him and waved him away angrily. Carlo hesitated, a worried look on his rugged face then reluctantly turned back to Felicianna and his brother Dante. Andrea Feltre watched him for a moment then began her tale once more.

In the days when "The Marches" were Papal dominions, the supreme families were the Sforzas, Matatestas, Feltres and the Molzas. Don Fabrizio Molza was young and handsome. Very tall they say, even taller than Carlo," they both looked over at Carlo who stood in heated conversation with Dante. "Well the Don had an eye for the women," Andrea continued. Just like Carlo thought Rita.

"But none of the mountain women seemed to satisfy him and he refused to marry. Which angered his father considerably," the old woman's eye traveled back to Carlo. The little flirtation with the college girls and Carlo flashed through Rita's mind.

"Do go on," she urged tearing her eyes from the tall powerful man who was speaking with such intensity that his older brother suddenly turned and fled the room.

"Well on the trip to Napoli the Don was bewitched by the lovely Countessa Anna Taranta. But she already had a husband and a very jealous mean spirited man he was. He would beat her when other men just looked her way. Her family refused to help her because the old Count was extremely wealthy and powerful. He would kill anyone to keep his beautiful young wife and some say he did several times. She was trapped in a hellish marriage. Until Don Fabrizio met her at dinner one night." Andrea took a small sip of her brandy then continued. "The old Count believed his beautiful Anna was kidnapped by the handsome Don Molza. He found an old Napoli witch and forced her to place a curse on the Molza family for generations to come. Then with his army marched towards Urbino to rescue Anna. But you see, dear, everyone knew that Anna was not carried off against her will. After all, she took her favorite ladies-in waiting, her favorite gowns and the fabulous Taranta jewels. No, it was a simple 'Affair of the Heart'." Andrea dabbed at her teary eyes.

"Yes the soldiers all knew and so rode slowly, laughing at the old Count. He died on the journey North a humiliated broken man. But, alas the old Count's sons by his first wife were only to happy to revenge their father. They wanted the jewels back in the family. It was not just the money value but a matter of honor. They did not raise an army to fight the brave Don Fabrizio, oh no instead they fought a deadly insidious war. They sent a bogus priest to assassinate the Don's beloved Cardinal Giorgio. Then several years later an evil witch of a murderess, the puttanta Serena stabbed to death the Don's young son.

Rita shook her head in disbelief. Unable to relate any of the sad story to her quiet life in Connecticut.

"Yes, Rita. Your own ancestors fought beside the Molzas," the old woman seemed to read Rita's mind. "The Don rode down from these mountains and his rage rolled through the streets of Napoli crushing all who were loyal to the Taranta family. Men, women and children all wiped from this earth."

Rita hung her head, "What a terrible massacre. What kind of people were they? How could they kill innocent children!" she felt very weary. She hated being in this mountain area. She just wanted to sell the Villa Sera and get back to a more civilized place like Connecticut. She wished that she had never inherited the Villa. Her eyes traveled back to Carlo still in deep conversation with Felicianna. His smile warm and sensual. He looked so relaxed. So loving and kind. But he is a Molza, she reflected, a direct descendant of the Don. No wonder he's so imperturbable and yet so volatile at times.

Andrea paused to sip her brandy daintily and then continued, "So over the years the legend has it that Anna, after her first born son was murdered, hid the fabulous jewels on the grounds of Villa Sera. She never wished to be reminded of the Tarantas and the terrible price she and the Don had paid for following their hearts. The jewels were never seen again."

"But what has this old history have to do with me?" Rita inquired still completely puzzled.

"You now own the Villa Sera," Andrea stated watching Rita closely.

"Oh. No. The lost jewels," Rita slumped back on the couch. She deeply resented being pulled back into this turbulent, emotional life. She thought she had left all this behind after that last summer at the Villa Sera with her laughing, suntanned parents. It was all coming back. She sensed more to this violent mystery. At least now she understood why none of them wanted her to sell the Villa.

"It's not just the jewels, Margarita," Aunt Andrea had a strange look in her eyes as she studied the younger woman. "The Bondones have owned Villa Sera for centuries. You are Margarita Bondone."

"Yes," Rita answered softly. She knew and had known all along she could not escape her heritage. She looked again at Carlo feeling childish and really stupid as she recalled lashing out at him for using her real name. Of course he would know it. Everyone here in Urbino knows my name. How could I have been such a silly fool!! She wished she could go back to this morning and start fresh with the tall handsome Carlo. If only she could erase the horror of the car chase. If only she could just remember Carlo's warm lips and forget the ugly past. She longed to walk over to where he stood with the lovely, shapely Felicianna and just apologize for being such a child. But just the way he looked at Felicianna told her he did not even know she was in the same room. Rita suddenly felt very lonely. Her head was spinning from all the history and family secrets. Her heart was heavy with the thought of her dashing parents so in love, so young to die. The past was beginning to close in on her again. She felt she must escape. She must go lie down in the quiet of her room. "Please excuse me Andrea. I think I'll go to my room. I feel awfully dizzy."

"Oh, but of course, my dear. How cruel of me to keep you so late when you have had such a trying day. Carlo. Carlo," she called, "please take Margarita to her room immediately. She's not feeling too well," Andre summoned Carlo with a dainty wave of her lace handkerchief Carlo was quickly by Rita's side, steadying her with a strong hand on her elbow.

"Certainly, I would be delighted to escort Margarita to her room," he really emphasized the "Margarita." Then briskly turned her out of the Library and up the wide staircase.

"I see Sofia has lit the lamps," he observed on opening the

bedroom door. "These old rooms can be frightening with all the dark shadows." Rita pulled away wondering if he was trying to scare her. She looked at his rugged face but he seemed to be genuinely concerned as he knelt to add more kindling to the fire glowing in the small fireplace. "This should hold you until morning."

Rita watched the muscles in his broad back as he stretched to place a heavy log on the fire. The spacious room was chilly and she hugged herself wishing she was back in her cozy Connecticut apartment with central heating.

Carlo stood, "It will take a few minutes but I think you will be comfortable enough." He brushed his hands on his pants. Rita was again conscious of how strong, how big he was. He towered over her a tall dark silhouette. She couldn't see his face clearly but his big frame was clearly outlined by the glowing fire behind him. She shivered partly from the cold but mostly from the sight of him standing there so close, so powerful. He had an aura of authority, a strong magnetism that drew her into his arms. She slipped her arms around his tapered waist and their lips met softly. A feeling of euphoria flowed through Rita's exhausted body. Her slender body pressed lightly, shyly against Carlo's solid frame. She hardly realized what she was doing. She had never known such warmth, such soothing tenderness She felt as if she were floating in a misty dream. Carlo ended the kiss and swept her up, carrying her to the large bed. As he placed her gently down on the covers, she reached eagerly for his lips and he returned her kiss with a much more passionate forceful kiss. She felt as if she were being consumed by his hot lips and she was helpless against their forceful demands. Just as the last remnant of her fragile resistance was about to surrender, Carlo straightened up. Ruffling her short blond hair, he whispered hoarsely, "Margarita, my sweet blond Americana, you have had too much wine and Sambuca tonight. You are lovely and very desirable but I think it's time I left. Buona notta, Margarita," and before she could protest he was gone.

As the fire blazed and crackled she drifted into a contented sleep with the memory of Carlo's warm lips on her. Dreamily she wondered what might have happened if Carlo had remained longer. Her dreams were warm and very pleasant and she slept through the whole night.

Chapter 5

The next day was sunny and warm as Rita breakfasted with Andre and Ernesto on the terrace.

"Father Vincenzo has returned to town and the de Sicas are late risers," volunteered a much more relaxed Ernesto. Well, he must have a lot of confidence in Carlo and the Inspectore, Rita thought as no mention was made of the strangers from the South. But Ernesto did not volunteer any information concerning the where abouts of the beautiful Felicianna. Nor Carlo. But he was only too happy to fill Rita in on the history of his own family, the Feltres.

"The Feltres settled their profitable paper-mill in the town of Farino in the late 12th century. The Feltre parchment became world known for its beauty and durability," he stated proudly. Rita's thoughts roamed as she tried to listen to Ernesto rambling on. Looking down to her right she saw a blue tiled rooftop poking up between the tall cypress trees.

"Villa Sera," she thought sadly. "Yes, I can remember vaguely that last summer. We came up here to the larger Villa San Giovanni for dinner that night." It had been a clear moonlit night and Rita had skipped along the winding path up the steep mountainside. The moon shadows cutting across the path were make-believe animals to chase. Father and Mother holding hands, running with her like two silly school-children. It was beginning to all come back, the past she had tried so hard to escape was insidiously enfolding her once again. The sound of tinkling crystal goblets, soft music and the laughter of a big happy family gathered together seemed to float out from the open French doors. Rita was amazed at how easily it all came back in a flash. For years she refused to think about that last summer. She had buried those memories so well that Aunt Andrea, Ernesto, the deSicas, and even Carlo had ceased to exist for her. Strange, she thought, why would I do such a thing?"

Being back here at Villa San Giovanni had released all those hidden memories. Now she could clearly picture that long ago dinner party. Aunt Louisa-Maria and Uncle Francesco presided over the long table. Rita clearly remembered sitting to her Aunt's right with her parents. Then her namesake her aunt Margarita with her gangling red-haired son Paul. On the other side of the food-laden table sat Ernesto, Aunt Andrea and a striking couple with a dark-haired young boy. She realized now that it must have been Carlo Molza and his parents. The dinner had been delicious with many courses served by the ever pleasant Barlettas. Rita was totally bewildered as to why she had buried such a happy memory. Her confused thoughts were interrupted by Andrea asking, "Margarita, are you listening? You look miles away. Please pay attention when I'm speaking. I'm really not used to your American manners!" her coffee cup struck the saucer with a sharp crack, reminding Rita of Louisa-Maria back in Boston snapping the stem of her crystal goblet.

"Oh, I'm so sorry Andrea. But I was just reminiscing about my last visit here. Remember when we all came up here to Villa San Giovanni for dinner. What a marvelous evening it was."

"Well of course I remember it was Festival time and Louisa-Maria always had a big crowd at Festival time," she glared impatiently at Rita, "but I was speaking to you about opening up Villa Sera and I do believe you did not hear one word I said." Andrea was very piqued with this strange American girl.

"Oh, Andrea. I'm so sorry." Rita was beginning to feel a warm bond towards the old woman. "Do forgive my rudeness. I know you want to help. But I had forgotten how really beautiful it is here. This gorgeous view. Those huge mountains," she gestured to the rugged Apennine mountains that rose majestically all around them. She felt lightheaded and slightly happy. The sun was warm on her bare arms and the smell of alpine roses, edelweiss; and gentians floated up from the gardens below the terrace. Yielding to the beauty of the day she turned to Andrea and said lightly, "Why don't I walk down to Villa Sera and look over the place?"

Suddenly it seemed a good idea to get away before Carlo and Felicanna showed up for breakfast. If they show up at all. He must have run right into her arms after kissing me good-night. She stood quickly not wanting the thought of Carlo in another woman's arms to spoil the lovely morning. She caught herself furiously brushing non-existing crumbs from her slacks. Embarrassed, she stopped abruptly.

"Ernesto will accompany you, Margarita," Andrea announced as she watched Rita curiously. Ernesto held up a large ring of keys.

"Off we go Margarita. Time to brush aside the cobwebs," he led the way down the stone terrace steps, across the wide green lawn and onto a narrow, winding path to Villa Sera.

It was late afternoon before they had completed their inspection of the Villa. It was a smaller version of the Villa above which they had just left. Situated a quarter of a mile down the mountainside, it was inaccessible by car. Supplies were brought down from the main Villa San Giovanni usually by donkey or horseback. The Villa clung to the lush mountainside, nestled among the tall cypress trees and almost invisible to the casual eye. Stone archways led out to the mosaic tiled terrazzo where Ernesto and Rita stood admiring the panoramic view of the twin mountain peaks. Soon, the sun would set directly between the snow-capped peaks leaving slashes of purple haze etched across the evening sky. A scene so breath-taking that the Villa had been named for the early evening haze which hung for hours delaying the fall of darkness.

"Villa Sera, evening home," Rita sighed, moved by the panoramic view she longed to stay for the sunset. But Ernesto would not hear of it. "The path is too rocky and treacherous and we did not think to bring a torchlight. It would be foolish to break an ankle. No, Margarita. Later when the Villa is opened you will have many beautiful sunsets to watch. Come, let us return." Ernesto turned back to the house. Thrilled by the view Rita hung back. Strange how they all expected her to reopen the Villa. Why couldn't they understand she had her own life to live in Connecticut. Lovely though the view was she sensed a harsh, turbulent under-current. Yes, she knew she would definitely sell the Villa. She hurried after Ernesto trying to shake the spell of belonging the Villa was weaving around her.

"Such foolishness. I don't need nor want an isolated mountainside villa," she slammed the heavy, beautifully carved door closed her hand caressing the rich dark wood. She froze for a moment hearing her father calling her name years ago on Festival night. Rita swirled around, her eyes searching every shadowy corner. She felt a chill sensing she should be hiding somewhere. But where. Her hands were clammy and she felt panic rising. She was paralyzed by some unknown fear.

"Margarita, over here," it was only Ernesto calling her from the side archway. The strange spell broke, freeing Rita from her icy terror. She cast one last frightened glance over her shoulder and hurried out into the garden.

"Look, Margarita over here. The Fountam of the Tortoises. I

had forgotten it was here. See how beautiful," he strolled around the small fountain.

"Oh, yes." Rita was thrilled. The fountain had been such a delight when she was a child. She reached over and patted the Dolphin which supported a young faun-boy reaching upwards to tip a squirming tortoise into the larger upper bowl of the fountain. The fountain was a copy of the much larger version in the Piazza Mattei. It was built for a young bride, homesick for her native Rome. Rita circled the fountain marveling at it's sweet enchanting effect. The marble was dry and cool. Dry leaves lay scattered in the two wide bowls. The nimble fauns looked ready to spring away once their task was completed. Ernesto was happily studying the intricate details as Rita completed her circle of the captivating fountain. A shaft of sunlight off to her right caught her eye. There, hidden in an overgrowth of shrubs sat the stone bench of her dreams.

"Oh, no," she half whispered, fear tightening her throat. A terrible sense of foreboding engulfing her. The horror of the constant nightmares washing over her, chilling her to the bone.

"Let's go, Ernesto. It's really getting dark," she hurried out of the garden. Running up the steep path she stumbled on the many loose stones strewn along the unused path. She was soon breathless and forced to slow down so Ernesto, puffing and panting could catch up.

"What's wrong Rita? Why did you run?" he asked worriedly.

"Oh, I don't know, Ernesto. I really can't explain. I don't

understand it myself. I guess I just wanted to get back. I am rather hungry. After all we did miss lunch," she answered lamely continuing to climb upwards leaving the strange little fountain and garden far behind.

"Yes, I'm so glad I ate a hearty breakfast. I had no idea we would be so long," puffed a tired Ernesto.

It was with immense relief that Rita found David Swan waiting on the terrace of Villa San Giovanni. After introducing Ernesto, who then left to dine with Father Vincenzo in town, she kissed David warmly.

"David how long have you been here? Why didn't they send someone to get us?" she hugged David happily.

"Whoa, girl. I've just arrived after an exhausting drive on a death defiling, cork-screw, bitch of a road," he ran his long hands through his sandy hair in exasperation.

Rita laughed, "Oh, David, you don't know just how bitchy. I've got so much to tell you. Come inside," they walked arms linked into the house, settling down in the Library.

"Now, love tell me all," David stretched his lanky body across the long couch cradling Rita in his long arms. By the time Rita had filled him in on the last few days beginning with the summons to Louisa-Maria's condo in Boston, to her brush with death on the mountain road and her quick inspection of the smaller Villa Sera, the quiet Sofia had brought them a supper tray and laid it on the corner game table. "Oh thank you Sofia. I am starved," Sofia informed them that Senora Feltre had retired earlier with a headache.

"Last night was too much excitement. Too much talk, too much Sambucca for an old woman like Senora Andrea," Sofia fussed about laying out the hot lentil soup, crusty bread with fresh mountain butter, a large spinach salad sprinkled with warm toasted bacon-bits and just enough lemon and oil dressing. She pointed out the bottles of tart greenish-white Verdicchio wine cooling on the sideboard. When she finally left, David and Rita poured the wine and toasted their evening together. Rita felt warm and happy. It was wonderful to have David here by her side. His blond, clean cut looks accentuated by his soft light blue shirt and dark navy pants helped to diminish her thoughts of the dark, brooding Carlo Molza. She desperately wanted to forget the hot feeling of his lips on hers. Forget the quick flame of desire his warm hands had ignited in her once calm breast. She studied David as he polished off his wine licking his straight lips in appreciation. She tried not to wonder why those lips had never demanded and searched so possessively as Carlo's had. She lowered her eyes to her soup even more determined to put Carlo Molza out of her mind, if not forever, at least for tonight.

They both ate heartily, pausing often to refill their wine glasses. The hot food revived Rita and she vowed not to skip lunch again. As they ate they talked or rather Rita talked of friends back in Connecticut. She realized most of them were her friends from work. She had never met any of David's friends. She attempted to get David to talk about his family and friends but he was very casual, turning the subject back to the sale of the Villa

Sera. Finishing the meal, they carried their wineglasses over to the rug in front of the fireplace. David threw some logs on and they stretched on the rug contentedly sipping the rest of the wine. Rita snuggled up close, nestling her head on David's shoulder.

"So you are really selling the Villa?" David asked lazily.

"Of course" Rita replied.

"How long will you be here?" he pressed his face into her soft blonde curls.

"I really don't know. Mr. Mattini, Andrea's lawyer said there would be no problems. He already has a buyer and the papers would only take a few days."

"That's not much time," David reflected.

"Well it's time enough for me. I can't wait to get away from here," she turned to give him a kiss but broke it off when she heard the door open and then close quickly. She glanced back at the large, heavy door.

"Did you hear that door open?"

"What door?" David murmured his head beginning to loll sleepily.

"Oh, nothing. I guess I'm just jumpy lately," she snuggled down again next to David's lanky frame. The wine was making her feel hot and feverish. Her body ached to be caressed. She pressed into David, wanting him to pull her close, to press their bodies together. But David's arms lay slack, his head thrown back, his mouth hanging open. He was fast asleep.

Chapter 6

A gentle, cool breeze wafting in from the lake awakened Rita early the next morning. Rising, she went to stand before the long French windows. She stretched her arms high over her head, gazing out at the undisturbed beauty of the mountains. The faint tinkle of the sheep-bells drew her gaze to the left, where high on the hillside a young boy was driving the small herd up the steep side. Higher and higher to the sweet smelling, abundant, green grass.

"I need some exercise," Rita decided, "a brisk jog to town and back will be just great, about four miles, perfect!" she calculated quickly.

She smiled happily as she threw on her pale yellow terri-cloth shorts and tank-top. Thick yellow ankle-socks were hastily pulled on and then one Adidas sneaker and a quick search for the other, which she finally found by the door where she had flung it at the retreating Carlo. The thought of the big, muscular man sent a shiver down her spine. She stood quickly, glanced at the pretty, blond in yellow staring back at her from the mirror. The trim, shapely body, barely covered by the brief shorts stood on long, trim legs. She grabbed a bright yellow head-band and pulled it over her short hair down onto her forehead. Rita felt exhilarated, energy flowed swiftly through her taut body.

"Maybe David will run today," she spoke aloud as she skipped happily out the door and down the corridor to David's door. She tapped lightly, "David?" Tapping harder she called a little louder, "David, let's take a run," still no answer.

"Oh, well, he's probably still tired after yesterday's flight and long drive. Plus, all that wine last night. It almost did me in too," she laughed to herself remembering her aching need for David the previous night.

"That cozy fire and sprawling on the floor. Oh, I'll have to be careful of that stuff," she blushed thinking of how shamelessly she had pressed closer and closer to David's lean body.

By now, she was well along the road to town. Jogging along at a steady pace, she skirted a large pothole in the road. Some village women walking to the hillside vineyards, screeched and shook their fists at her. Their dark, black dresses and shawls resembling a flock of cackling crows.

Rita ignored their taunts, her mind still on the night before.

"Yes," she thought "Dear, sweet David. His big, blue eyes had sure closed quickly after a few glasses of wine. Not exactly what she had wanted at that moment but now in the bright, early morning sunlight she realized it was all for the best. She had been really lucky, to be saved from her own weak flesh. She thought fondly of David. She never felt threatened around him. He was always cool, completely in control of his emotions.

So engrossed had she been in memories of David and last night that she had failed to hear the truck which was now almost upon her. As it drew alongside her, three rough-looking, mountain men standing in the back began yelling at her. She smiled and waved, wishing her Italian was better. The men grinned broadly, the larger one turned and pounded on the cab of the truck, which disappeared in a whirl of dust around the bend in the winding road. Rita stumbled over a large rock, her vision obscured by the whirling dust.

"Rats, these mountain roads are really rotten!" A steep drop fell off not two feet from where she stood, rubbing her sore ankle. She looked warily down the mountainside.

"Hmm, a bit different from Storrow Drive back in Boston."

She started jogging cautiously down the winding road. Her ankle was beginning to ache and she doubted she could make it to town and back. She rounded the bend and was about to turn back when she saw the truck stopped with the three rough-looking men standing beside it. She realized, then, that this truck was the only traffic she had seen on this lonely, quiet mountain road Feeling just a little apprehensive, she tried to make a quick U-turn but the big man was waving his hands and grinning. She thought, with her limited Italian, that he was offering her a lift into town.

"Gracie, no thank you," she smiled, shaking her head. She tried to pass but the tall one grabbed her arm, pulling her close to him. She could smell the wine on his breath, see the wine stains on his rough, brown shirt. He smiled broadly his thick, red tongue flickered over his black, bushy moustache.

"Luigi, no. No, Americana!" the smaller man stepped toward them. It was then, seeing the worry on his face that Rita went cold. Fear gripped her, making her nauseous. She couldn't believe what was happening. The giant of a man was speaking to her as he held her close. His voice was low and gutteral, his dark eyes feverish, his big peasant hands pressed on her lower back bringing their bodies together in a quick thrust. Rita felt the enormous hardness of him and she screamed in panic

"No, no let me go, you idiot!" she pounded her fists on the huge shoulders. Her squirming and fighting seemed to excite the big man even more. He bellowed happily and lifted her off her feet. Pressing and rubbing her pelvis up and down his pants over his bulging hardness. Rita was hysterical, scarcely able to believe what was about to happen to her. She tried to reach his face to scratch him with her long nails but he pinned her arm painfully behind her back. She could feel her shorts being pulled down from the rear and she screamed and pleaded.

Suddenly there was a loud screech of tires and an angry voice rang out over her cries. The giant dropped her abruptly and she fell in a pitiful heap at his feet.

"Get Up!" icy voice commanded.

She stood quickly on her shaking feet and hurried towards the voice. Raising her eyes, she looked into the frozen face of Carlo Molza. His dark eyes blazed with fury.

"Get in the car," he snarled. His eyes not leaving the two men.

The smaller man came forward timidly, removing his hat, his hands out pleading, he spoke in a shaking voice.

"Is not Luigi's fault, Mr. Molza. The Americana, she smile, she wave. He not know. He not listen to me. I try to tell him but he say she ready. She ready," he looked pleadingly at Carlo, who took a step closer, clenching his fists.

"No, no, please, Mr. Molza. Luigi don't understand about Americana women—she is the first one he ever see," the small man backed way from Carlo, wringing his hat in his hands.

Carlo stepped closer to the men, a burst of Italian sprang from his tight lips, his voice icy cold. His right hand slipped inside his jacket and Rita was stunned, as through her tears she saw all the three men fall to their knees. They pleaded frantically with Carlo, who towered over them, staring coldy at their bowed heads. After, several, long moments, Carlo turned quickly and strolled back to the car. Not even looking at Rita, he raced the engine and spun them away down the mountain.

Rita could feel his anger filling the small car. He drove swiftly, taking great liberties on some of the sharp curves. Finally Rita was able to stop crying and shaking. She turned a tear-stained face towards the angry Carlo.

"Thank you, Carlo. I was very lucky you came along," she could barely choke out the tremulous words.

"Stupido. You American women really are something. You run around half-naked then…"

"I'm not half-naked," she was shocked at the venom in his cold voice. "This is a jogging suit," she added lamely, looking down at her skimpy yellow shorts.

"Well, this is not Boston, Massachusetts. You are in the mountains of Italy. A place not quite caught up to the twentieth century. How could you be so stupid. Look at you, for God's sake," he glared at her furiously.

Rita began to shake again only this time from anger not fear.

"How dare you insinuate I provoked that assault. You are a backwards, chauvinistic bastard," she spat the words at him. The next minute she was thrown against him when he suddenly pulled the Maserti to a quick stop off the road. Carlo grabbed her arms, pulling her close, he pinned her in front of him.

"Don't call me names, you American bitch," his hands bit painfully into her soft arms. His dark eyes bore into her, hard and brittle.

"I saw you last night in the library with your all-American boy You looked like you were enjoying every minute!" he drew her tight, kissing her fiercely, forcing his hot tongue into her unyielding mouth.

"Oh, no," Rita thought desperately. Carlo had the wrong idea. She tried to pull away but he tightened his grip. His hands like steel bands cutting into her arms. His lips pressed her head back painfully and she felt tears spring to her eyes. Finally, she stopped all efforts to fight him off. She was too exhausted physically and emotionally to cope with this mixed up problem. In her confused mind she knew that it was important that Carlo know she wasn't what he thought she was. She wanted very much to have him understand but she could tell by his violent kisses that, now, was not the time to try and explain anything. His rage was inflamed to the breaking point.

She let herself go slack in his grip. Carlo feeling her body go limp, ceased his brutal kiss and pushed her to the other side of the car.

"Why did you come back? Why didn't you stay in America?" his voice was heavy with anguish and he punched the steering wheel with the heel of his right hand.

"Please, Carlo, take me back to the Villa," she felt drained and bruised. Her body ached all over. Her ankle now throbbed painfully, her ribs felt sore where the giant Luigi had lifted her off her feet, and, now, her upper arms and lips hurt because of Carlo's sudden assault. She felt truly naked and somehow lost. Everything was happening so fast. Here in Urbino she was all mixed up. She just wanted to get the sale over with and get back home to Connecticut.

She looked over at Carlo's handsome profile as he manuvered the small car around and back towards the Villa San Giovanni. Her arms ached painfully where he'd held her so forcefully and her lips felt crushed and bruised. She should hate him, she thought, but for some strange reason, she desperately wanted him to understand about David and last night. Also, this ugly incident this morning.

"Carlo, about last night..." she began timidly.

"Please. Spare me the hot details!" he snarled.

Rita felt frustrated and hurt at his attitude but she tried again. "But David and I never..."

"Look, baby, I've been there. I don't need a road map! Soft rug, blazing fire, wine and a willing lady," he leered at her his dark eyes raking her trembling body.

"Nothing happened," she protested angrily. Then wanted to bite her tongue. "Damn," she thought, 'I don't owe him an explanation. What am I doing? Who does he think he is? What a spineless ass I am,' she suddenly was ashamed of herself. She turned on him.

"Well, what about you and Felicianna? Where were you all night and all day?" she hissed at him.

Carlo's answer was a scathing look then stony silence for the rest of the ride back to the Villa.

Rita felt even more flustered when David met them on the steps of the Villa. Hastily, she made the introductions, feeling all the while very embarrassed standing in her torn yellow shorts between the two, tall, handsome men. David's gaze kept lingering on the dark marks appearing on her upper arms. His blue eyes questioned her silently. Rita felt totally vulnerable looking up at the two men, who stood eye to eye in quiet confrontation.

"Excuse me, but I really must go change," she had to get away from both of them. She needed to be alone in order to get her thoughts back together again. Nodding slightly, she dashed to her room. Glad to be free from the strong animosity that had sprung up so quickly between David and Carlo.

Chapter 7

After soaking in the tub for an hour, Rita felt somewhat better. She splashed cold water on her face and it seemed to help revive her natural good looks and restore her depressed spirits. Slipping into a light, long-sleeved Indian muslin dress with intricate embroidery on the scoop neck and long cuffs, she noticed the ugly bruises appearing on her arms.

"Damn that Carlo," she cursed the dark, intense stranger who had come into her life and awakened feelings too perplexing for her tired body and mind too handle. She grabbed a brush and began stroking her short, blond curls in quick, furious jabs. Annoyed at her thoughts of Carlo, she decided to call Domenic Mattini immediately and advise him to go ahead with the sale of Villa Sera. After talking with the lawyer in Rome, Rita felt elated. Soon she would be free of Urbino, free of the past, and far away from these rugged mountains and most of all far away from the volatile Carlo Molza.

Luncheon was served on the Terrace. Three large, blue and white umbrellas shaded three round tables clustered at the far end. Rita joined David under one and was surprised to find Carlo sitting, complacently sipping a tall vodka and tonic. David gave her a quick kiss on the cheek and then turned his attention to Ernesto and their conversation about a rare, missing Raphael madonna. Urbino was the birthplace of the famous painter and rumor had it that one of his earliest paintings was lost somewhere in the rambling, mountain town. Rita looked up to find Carlo staring coldly at her. Uncomfortable under his cold glare, she turned to Felicianna seated beside her. She was determined not to let Carlo disturb her composure again.

Felicianna was truly beautiful and Rita regarded the woman with open admiration.

'What a great subject, with her high cheek bones and large, dark eyes. I must sketch her sometime,' she thought as Felicianna chatted on about her own villa. Rita realized that villas were the number one topic of conversation this week-end. She was, also, surprised to hear a young person such as Felicianna speak with such love and pride about Urbino. Rita had thought only the older generation was involved in preserving these old Villas. Yet, the beautiful, young woman was speaking enthusiastically about restoring her family Villa, to carefully preserving arches, pillars and ancient tile work. Rita was drawn to Felicianna's warm, earthy manner. She found she was beginning to like the striking young woman. By the time lunch was over Rita had accepted

Felicianna's invitation to dine the next evening at the Villa Portinari.

At the next table, Father Vincenzo rose, extended his arms to include the whole luncheon group. "And now, my dear friends, it will be my honor and privilege to guide you through our lovely city, Urbino, jewel of the Marches."

As they trooped out to the cars, Rita was relieved to find that she and David would lead the way with Father Vincenzo, while Carlo tagged along behind, alone in the Masserati. Felicianna rode with Dante and the deSicas bringing up the rear.

Father Vincenzo turned out to be an expert guide. He knew all the hidden attractions as well as the more famous ones. Some of the narrow streets were just a series of stairs that the elderly priest led them tirelessly up and down. The city was early Renaissance, beautiful at every turn. The Church of San Giovanni, where they now stood, looked out across the hills to the Ducal Palace, whose twin towers, massive walls and many loggias filled the mountainside. Ancient and impressive.

"Built by our beloved Duke Federigo Montefeltro. A true 'Condottiere,' war lord," explained Father Vincenzo. "We will visit the Ducal Palace and the Black Marble Tombs another day," and he turned back to hurry into the Church of San Giovanni. Rita hastened after him, eager to question him about the Tombs.

Inside was dark and musty. The altar candles cast long shadows, Father Vincenzo was stopping in front of a large fresco depicting the Crucifixion.

"Painted by the Salimbeni brothers, who were local artists from San Severino," he stated proudly.

Even in the dim light Rita could appreciate the soft, lovely colors.

"And, here on each side-wall, we have the life of Saint John the Baptist. Quite an eyeful, eh?" he smiled broadly, immensely pleased with his church.

Rita marveled at the artist's control of light and color. The dark sides of his forms were illuminated with reflected light, thus avoiding heavy shadows. The figure of Saint John, the Baptist, stood with towering fury over the worldly, indifferent crowd milling about at the base of the frescoe. The artist's skillful use of the triangular setting conveyed clearly to the viewer the urgency of Saint John's message of the future coming of Christ. Rita closely studied the magnificent frescoe. She was thrilled that this visit to Urbino could be put to some good, artistic use. Finally, she allowed the unhappy David to drag her outside to join the group again.

"Now, I believe we have time to visit Raphael's birthplace," Father Vincenzo said as he glanced at his wristwatch and David perked back to life.

After driving a short, twisting route, they soon stopped on a steep hill in front of a tall house, similar to all the others but with a small plaque displayed on the wall. Inside, the kitchen, patio, and bedrooms were simple and unadorned. Rita marvelled that a genius such as Rafael began his life in such unassuming quarters.

She thought of his tranquil madonnas. His paintings were so ideally beautiful and peaceful, she wondered how he could have expressed such a graceful, spiritual beauty when he lived high in these wild, rugged mountains.

As they drove away, Rita glanced back. She gasped in wonder for there behind her was a true Rafael landscape. The mountains soaring above the vineyards, patches of red, blue and yellow flowers dotting the landscape. A quiet, pastoral scene worthy of a Rafael.

Father Vincenzo dropped them back at Villa San Giovanni and then sped back down the mountain as the sun settled low between the twin mountain peaks.

"Let's go out on the terrace and watch the sun set," David suggested, putting his arm around Rita. Strolling through the foyer they met Sofia with a tray laden with Champagne filled glasses. Laughing conspiritorily, they each snatched a glass, slipped by the library door, where they spied everyone gathered near the fire.

Out on the terrace, the scene was majestic as the sun set in a blaze of orange and yellow. Rita and David sipped their Champagne in silence. After a few moments, Rita realized she was chilled as her thin muslin dress blew in the cool mountain breeze. She thought she saw a light flicker once down on the path to Villa Sera and she shivered thinking of the dark shadows that had surrounded her in the strange, little garden with the fountain of the Tortoises.

"Oh, you are cold," David turned from her placing his glass on one of the round tables. "I'll get you a wrap."

Rita turned slightly to protest, "No, let's go…" she heard a loud crack and felt a searing pain on the side of her head. Then all was blackness.

Chapter 8

Rita opened her eyes slowly, the pain on the right side of her head seemed unbearable. She reached up with her right hand and discovered her forehead was heavily bandaged. She tried to speak but her mouth was dry and speech failed her. Father Vincenzo leaned over her, gesturing to a dark figure behind him, he spoke soothingly.

"Relax, my dear. You are safe now," the other figure handed the priest a glass which he raised to Rita's dry lips.

"I returned as soon as I heard," he explained as she sipped the cool water gratefully. The effort bringing sharp stabbing pains to her right temple. She moaned and lay back closing her eyes tightly.

"What has happened?" she whispered hoarsely. Several voices spoke excitedly. Rita tried opening her eyes again. Her vision was badly blurred. She could see Father Vincenzo when he leaned close but the rest of the room remained in gray darkness. Rita sensed others in the room but couldn't tell who they were.

"David, David," she cried remembering her last sight was of the lanky, blond American.

"I'm here, Rita," his tall form replaced Father Vincenzo. "You were shot at," he said bluntly, "Luckily, we both had turned or…" he patted her shoulder.

"Oh, my God!" Rita began sobbing. A strange voice ordered everyone out of the room. Then Father Vincenzo spoke gently in her left ear, "Margarita, Doctor Cuneo is going to give you a shot." Immediately she felt a quick prick on her right arm. "It will help you relax and sleep for a while. Carlo has a man stationed outside the door so you needn't worry about a thing," he spoke reassuringly, and Rita lulled by his voice and the mild tranquilizer drifted off peacefully.

When she awoke later, sunlight filtered through the closed drapes. She looked slowly around the room being careful not to move her aching head. Although the pain was much improved from last night, her vision in her right eye was very poor. She lay very still. Too frightened to even think. Tears trickled down her pale cheeks as she heard the door open and someone entered but all she could make out was a tall form coming towards her.

"No…Please…No,"Rita pleaded, desperately afraid it was her mysterious assailant returning. She tried to rise but strong hands pushed her gently back on the bed.

"Margarita, don't be afraid. It's me, Carlo," he spoke firmly.

Caressing her shoulders until she relaxed. Rita opened her terror-filled eyes to find Carlo's warm, dark eyes studying her face.

"You will be all right. Do you understand me?" he inquired gently.

Rita licked her dry lips, "Yes," she managed to croak softly.

"Wait, don't talk yet," he left and returned with some cool water, which Rita gulped down. She felt as if she were burning up. She moaned and moved her head restlessly

"Why? Why, Carlo? I don't understand why anyone would want to kill me?" the tears flowed down her cheeks. Carlo gently wiped them away and kissed her softly on her parched lips.

"I don't know either, Rita, but I'm going to damn well find out," he assured her. She stared at him and her heart ached. She longed to reach out to him, to be held safe and warm in his strong arms. He moved away a bit and she clutched his sleeve, afraid he would leave her alone again. He caught a glimpse of the bruises on her arm. Bruises his strong hands had made the previous morning.

"Oh, God," he leaned to kiss her arm, "Rita, I'm sorry. I'm sorry. I never meant to hurt you. Forgive me, please?" he pleaded.

"Oh, Carlo. There's nothing to forgive. We were both so wrong. I was jealous of you and Felicianna, so I called you those awful names," her throat ached from the effort of speaking.

Carlo kissed her dry lips, soothing them with his wet tongue.

"No, darling. I reacted badly. I went crazy when I saw that big oaf holding you up like that, so helplessly. You are just too beautiful to be running around these mountains in tiny, yellow shorts," he kissed her lightly, then straightened up.

"Darling, I have to go."

"No, no, please stay," Rita clung to his arm.

"I must talk to Inspectore Adolfo. We must get to the bottom of this shooting. In the mean time, you will be safe here. Trust me, Margarita. I have men posted around the Villa. You should rest. Andrea will be in shortly. She really blames herself for all this."

"Blames herself? But why?"

"Who knows, darling. Now rest. I'll be back before you know it." Carlo left, stopping to give orders to someone outside the bedroom door. Rita drifted in and out of sleep, sometimes bits of her strange dream tormented her rest. Visions of the graceful fountain of the Tortoises, the shadowy, stone bench with the hooded, seated figures, bright, shiny objects whirling around in the gray mist always just out of her reach.

She woke with a start. Andrea sat quietly beside the bed. Her thin, veined hand lay atop Rita's fevered brow.

"You were having a bad dream, my dear."

"Oh, yes, I have it often," Rita replied.

"Have it often?" questioned the old woman, a worried frown on her sweet, lined face.

"Yes, it is always the same dream or I should say nightmare," Rita sighed.

"Tell me about it then, dear. Maybe we can exorcise it by

talking about it," Andrea made herself comfortable in the small, bedside chair.

Rita began slowly and painfully describing the strange, haunting dream to her Aunt, who would give her occasional sips of luke-warm tea. As the tale of the blood running over her feet, across the blue mosaic tile, unfolded, Andrea replaced the teacup on the breakfast tray. She drew the ever-present lace handkerchief from her sleeve and wiped the tears from her eyes. The gesture reminded Rita, again, of her other Aunt back in Boston. How alike they are, she thought, and how very much she missed home.

"Please, Andrea, it's only a dream. I can handle it," Rita stated, not too bravely, thinking of the other afternoon down at Villa Sera, when she had heard voices calling her name.

"Oh, my dear. I had no idea you were suffering so. I told Louisa-Maria that we should have talked to you about that night. You were so young. But your father swore us to silence," Andrea sobbed into her hands. Rita started to get sharp pains shooting in her head again. She was puzzled by Andrea's words. It was so hard for her to think clearly. Something kept pushing at the fringes of her conciousness. The harder she tried to remember the more confused she became.

"Andrea, please, what night? What about my father?" she pleaded with the old woman but Andrea sat quietly sobbing. Her sobs finally lulling Rita back into a fitful sleep.

The next time she woke, Rita was ravenous. She sat up

carefully, her head pains just a bearable headache. As she debated trying to walk to the bathroom, Sofia entered carrying a tray emitting delicious aromas. Behind her came Doctor Cuneo, Father Vincenzo, and Carlo.

"So the patient feels better, I see," exclaimed the Doctor. He approached the bed and examined Rita. Waving a tiny flashlight into her eyes. He grunted and nodded affirmatively.

"Yes, my dear young lady, you were very fortunate indeed. The bullet just grazed your right temple, but you did suffer a mild concussion when you fell forward, hitting your head on the table. A few days of complete rest and you'll be fit as a fiddle." Doctor Cuneo snapped his black bag shut. "I'll be back next week. Until then, remember rest, rest and more rest," he rose, nodded to Carlo and Father Vincenzo and left.

Sofia placed the luncheon tray before Rita. A small bouquet of purple and white violets nosed shyly from a tiny straw basket, a deep purple, linen napkin lay beside a steaming bowl of rich Minestrone soup, thick chunks of garden fresh vegetables floated in the pinky, tomato broth. Beside the soup, a delicate small loaf of Sofia's freshly baked wheat bread, with a sparkling white crock-pot filled with the sweet, mountain butter. While a matching white tea-pot steamed thin whisps of aromatic tea. Rita ate hungarily as Father Vincenzo and Carlo related what they had learned from the Polizia.

Apparently the black Alfretta had been registered in Rome to a notorious mobster. But had been reported stolen a week ago.

The two, dead men had long criminal records with ties to a terrorist group, the Tre-Scalini. Why they attempted to push Carlo and Rita off the mountain road was still a mystery.

"Do you think it has something to do with selling the Villa Sera?" Rita asked.

The two men exchanged quick glances.

"Well, my dear, I don't see why. There have been many Villas sold over the last five years," Father Vincenzo replied lamely, "maybe it was a case of mistaken identity," he added looking hopefully at Carlo.

"But the shooting...you don't mean David? They were shooting at David?" Rita knew how ludicrous that sounded. She looked at Carlo, his face was a cold mask, his eyes dark and hostile. She sank back on the pillows, exhausted and dizzy from sitting up so long to eat. She stared at Carlo's rigid, blank face and thought of David. His blond, handsome face, the last sight she saw before she blacked out. Was that a step back he took? Oh, no! She remembered she had reached out to him for support but he had stepped back. Why hadn't he caught her as she fell forward, maybe she wouldn't have hit her head on that table if he had caught her.

"Oh, no," she moaned aloud, her face reflecting her inner turmoil.

"Margarita, it doesn't matter," Carlo leaned forward to take her hands in his.

"What doesn't matter?" Rita thought painfully. She looked

into Carlo's rugged, tanned face. His dark eyes were warm and caring.

'He knows,' Rita thought shocked at the realization. 'He knows, somehow, that David let me fall,' she pulled her hand free from Carlo's firm grasp and rubbed her forehead. 'Oh, no, I must not believe that. I'm going crazy. Not David. No,' she pushed violently on Carlo's broad chest.

"Everything matters," she replied annoyed at herself for such thoughts. Her blue eyes flashed angrily back at Carlo. "Someone has tried to kill me! Not once but twice. That certainly matters to me."

"But, of course I did not mean that," Carlo agreed quickly, concealing his hurt. "Well," he jumped to his feet and walked briskly to the door, "I'll be seeing my father this afternoon, so we should have some solid facts to work with then, until this evening…" a curt nod to Father Vincenzo and not a glance at Rita.

Rita closed her eyes in exasperation, "Nothing ever turns out right with that man," she fumed.

Seconds later, David strolled in. He looked neat and clean-cut in light blue casual slacks and white open-neck shirt. He kissed her cheek, shook hands with Father Vincenzo and sat on the edge of the bed. His bright, blue eyes gleamed happily.

"So, you'll be up and around in no time, Darling. No harm done," he patted her hand casually, "You look fine, Rita," he grinned at her.

"Thank you, David." She felt hurt at his casual tone. She studied his bright eyes. Eyes that registered none of the worry, concern or caring that Carlo's dark eyes had filled with as he looked at her.

David turned blithely to Father Vincenzo and proceeded to discuss the Ducal Palace. He was extremely interested in the history of the Montefeltros. Rita listened to their talk for awhile, growing increasingly annoyed with David's blase attitude towards the attempt on her life.

When finally she couldn't stand it a minute more, she interrupted them, "David, why didn't you catch me?"

"Waa—what dear?' David turned slowly back to Rita.

"I said, why didn't you catch me?" Rita enunciated each word carefully. "You were close enough, I know, I reached for you for support," she stated flatly.

"Oh, Lord, Rita. It happened so fast," he looked apologetically at Father Vincenzo, spreading his hands helplessly, he continued, "You know, I would have if at all possible. I was stunned. You fell so quickly. Hell, Rita, who the hell expects to get shot at on their vacation," he gathered her in his arms. Kissing her lightly, he smelled of 'Aqua Velvet,' his skin smooth and firm.

Rita hugged him back, 'Yes, he's right, of course,' she thought, the shock, the suddeness, it was natural he'd be frightened too. Stunned into immobility, that would account for his failure to prevent her falling.

Father Vincenzo coughed discreetly and they broke apart, grinning happily.

"I'm riding to Loreto this afternoon, David. It's a pilgrimage day and I've promised Father Bosco to help greet the trains of sick arriving every hour. If you'd like to join me, I would be happy for the company."

"Certainly, Father, I have heard a lot about Loreto. It would be my pleasure," David answered eagerly.

When they had left, Rita tried to rest but her mind was in a turmoil. She wondered why Carlo's father, who she hardly knew, would have information on her mysterious assailant. When Sofia came to remove her luncheon tray, Rita asked her that very question.

"Oh, signorina, Mr. Molza is the number one, 'uomo ripeattato' of these mountains. He is a very great man. A man much respected. He will solve this nasty mess," Sofia nodded her head vigorously.

"All is known to Signore Molza. You will see. Do not worry, my dear. The Molzas will take good care of you," she stated emphatically.

"You mean, Mr. Molza and his two sons, Carlo and Dante?" Rita wondered if there were any more Molzas around.

Sofia stopped at the door, she looked steadily at Rita,

"Especially, Carlo," she answered softly, turning and leaving.

Rita to ponder a new thought, 'especially Carlo?' When she finally did fall asleep, Rita dreamed of Carlo, bathing her feverish brow, moistening her parched lips with his sensual, wet tongue. The image wavered and changed to David with his crystal, blue eyes and dry, cool lips. Rita thrashed around trying to escape them both. She ran down the smooth, moon-lit path into the garden, where she saw her father grappling with a dark shape, they were struggling violently and the dark shape fell striking its head on the edge of the marble fountain. Rita ran towards her father, she was a young girl, again, with her long golden hair streaming behind her.

"Papa, Papa," she cried throwing herself into his trembling arms.

She glanced down as a warmness spread over her pretty, white sandals. A piercing scream tore from her throat. Pulling away from her father, she did a crazy tap dance on the blue, mosaic tiles trying desperately to escape the ribbon of blood seeping from the dark shape lying near the fountain of the Tortoises.

"Magarita, mia bambina!" her father cried out reaching for her as she whirled around and around. She was frantic to escape the blood covering her pretty, white sandals. Turning, she raced sobbing back up the path to the Villa San Giovanni, high above her, ablaze with bright lights.

Rita awoke from the tortuous nightmare in a cold sweat. She lay rigid in her damp bed. Now, she remembered why she had never wanted to return to Villa Sera. That terrible night. That moon-lit night when in the garden of the Tortoises she had seen her beloved father kill a man. Rita unconsciously began wiping one foot with the other. Over and over. Wipe away the horror. Wipe away the blood. Wipe, wipe, wipe. Finally the rigid dam broke and she wept as she had never wept before. It was true, the Bondones were cursed. All had the taint of spilled blood. Even her own parents. She cried until there were no tears left and her feet ceased their useless wiping. Exhausted, she slipped into a deep dreamless sleep.

Chapter 9

The next morning, Rita felt remarkably fit. It was as if a heavy weight had been lifted from her thin shoulders. The past would always be with her but the dark fears, the unknown terrors she had experienced as a child could now be put into perspective. She wrote a long letter to Louisa-Maria, explaining how her fall was causing her dreams to become clearer. She did not mention the shooting, for fear of upsetting the old woman. Rita then wrote to her office asking to prolong her vacation, and then to several dear friends. She paused in her writing, strange, now that she thought about it but David had never introduced her to any of his old friends. Everyone they saw socially were friends of hers. Yes, David was very reserved. But, that was what had drawn her to him after her fiancée was killed. She had never wanted to be rushed. And David certainly respected her wishes. She wished she could see him right now. She was no longer annoyed at his indifferent behavior putting it off to his reluctance for demonstrative affections. Wondering how he was doing with Father Vincenzo in Loreto, she picked up her small hand mirror.

"Well, David's off tending to sick pilgrims and I lie here with a shiner! When he gets back tomorrow I will be up and around and we will have a nice, long talk," she decided firmly.

"Quite a shiner, you have there," a deep, familiar voice caught her unawares. She quickly put down the mirror and watched Carlo stroll into the room. He stood over her, ruggedly handsome in fresh faded denims. His big shoulders and arms bulging in a bright, red shirt.

"I'll have Sofia send something up for that beauty," he peered closely at her eye.

"Don't bother. I can take care of it myself."

"So I see," he laughed indulgently. Then in a more serious tone, "How's your vision?"

"Much better, thank you," she answered sheepishly. She found it hard to be indifferent to this dark, caring man. His touch was warm and strong as he gently turned her head examining her eye. Satisfied, he sat back on the edge of the bed.

Rita instinctively moved her legs slightly away from his body but Carlo reached over and drew her legs back, his hand moving slowly up her thigh stopping possessively on her hip. He leaned forward and kissed her firmly on the lips, still caressing her hip he spoke in his low, husky voice.

"We know who hired the men in the black Alfetta," Rita stiffened, waiting anxiously for Carlo to continue.

"Donato Cigno," Carlo watched her closely. Rita stared blankly back.

"Nothing," she whispered, "Nothing. It means nothing to me," tears brimmed her eyes. "Oh, Carlo, why would a complete stranger want me dead?" she cried.

"Well, not a complete stranger to the family," Carlo remarked cautiously. His strong, large hand kneaded her hip. The warm, dark eyes searching her face.

"Margarita, do you remember years ago when you were just a child, there was an accident at the Villa Sera involving your father and another man?"

Rita looked deeply into the dark eyes watching her with troubled concern and at that moment she loved him for his gentle, kindness.

"You mean a murder, Carlo?"

He removed his hand from her hip, clasping the big hands between his knees, his dark head bent forward. "So, you do remember?" his voice was flat, expressionless.

"Not until last night. For years, I've been plagued by nightmares. I guess coming here, being shot at, the concussion, all helped to restore memories I wanted kept hidden," she put her hand over his clenched fists. He turned pulling her into his wide chest. He held her close, kissing her soft, blond hair.

"Margarita, I couldn't believe you were really coming back. I thought I would never see you again. I, too, have been haunted by that awful night. The sight of you running, screaming up the path, your beautiful, blond hair streaming behind you. I tried to hold you, I wanted to calm you, protect you but they all came running out, they pulled us apart and carried you into the Villa. Oh, Margarita, my love," he pressed a kiss to her lips. A long, passionate kiss that breached years of longing. Rita felt herself surrendering to the warmth, the gentle kindness, then suddenly the terrible scene in the garden flashed through her dazed mind.

'Oh, no,' she thought desperately, 'I don't want to be a part of all this. I've my own life in Connecticut, far from this madness,' she broke off the kiss, turning her face from his puzzled look.

"What is it, darling?"

"Please, Carlo, I must think. And, there is David too, remember?"

"Yes, of course, David. Your clean-cut American boy." he snarled.

"Oh, stop calling him that. He's not a boy, he's a man," she snapped back.

"I doubt that," Carlo reiterated softly, his voice like steel.

"Well, forget David. Tell me about this Donate, what's his name. Does he want Villa Sera? I'll sell it to him, he doesn't have to kill me for it," Rita protested, sitting up defiantly, her black eye beginning to throb.

"Well, my dear girl, it's far more complicated," Carlo answered sharply.

"Well, tell me. I'm not altogether stupid as you seem to think." She was close to tears, wondering how they had gone from loving to fighting so, quickly.

"No, but you HAVE forgotten your heritage!" he turned and strode swiftly out of the room.

"Beast!" Rita screamed and flung a pillow at the empty doorway. A huge, burly man appeared, stooped to recover the pillow and return it to Rita with a shy, smile.

"Grazie, thank you," she murmured meekly. It was her first sight of the guards Father Vincenzo had spoken about.

Chapter 10

Aunt Andrea and Sofia flatly refused to allow Rita to get out of bed until Doctor Cuneo returned to examine her. So, Rita filled the long hours reading about The Marches, that wide range of vast mountains towering up and down the Adriatic side of Italy. It was a very rugged country that bred tough, rebellious people. As she read she thought often of Carlo Molza. She was beginning to understand him. She had to admit that he had been right. She never should have gone out jogging alone in this isolated mountain area. Just thinking of those three rough truckers brought shivers to her spine. She would certainly have been raped if it hadn't been for Carlo. She accepted some of the blame, she knew, now, that here in The Marches things were a lot different.

"Heavens," she sighed, "I'm back in the Middle Ages." Picking up her book again, she was soon absorbed in the life of the Duke Federigo Montefeltro, the great "Condottiere" warlord, of Urbino. The Duke was a clever tactitian and won many battles but it was his inquiring mind that fascinated Rita. Duke Montefeltro established a vast library covering a multitude of subjects such as medicine, physics, theology, architecture, history, poetry and religion. He found time to help the local people by educating the poorer boys and providing dowries for the poorer girls. He was a kind, generous leader and Rita felt she was reading about her own grandfather, Aldo Bondone. He, too, had ruled Urbino, as Mayor, years ago, also with a firm and loving hand. Her thoughts roamed back to her early childhood at Villa Sera. How proud her father was of the Villa, which had been in the family for hundreds of years. The three of them had been so happy there. She looked out the window, far down the mountside, she could see patches of the blue-tiled roof of the Villa Sera.

"Maybe I SHOULD keep the Villa for a little longer. It's so lovely here," she gazed across at the snow capped mountains. A blackbird swooped from the tall cypress outside the window and flashed by, it's harsh cackle filling her with trepidation. She wondered if it was an omen warning her. Warning her to stay away from Urbino just as the mysterious caller in Rome had warned her. Rita shut the book and reached for her sketchpad.

"Better to dwell on the present and forget the past," she admonished herself, and she began a small drawing of the beautiful twin mountain peaks soaring above the valley visible from her bedside window.

Every day Andrea would find a minute to stop in on Rita. They never mentioned that moonlit night in the garden, again. The kind old woman would fill Rita with tales of the local families, who was marrying whom, which new bride was expecting and which poor wife was unfortunately not to be expecting. Rita smiled patiently at her Aunt's references to her single status, she had heard the same remarks from Louisa-Maria back in Boston. Right now, Rita reflected, marriage was the least of her worries. There was still someone out there trying to kill her and that thought was always intruding into her daily thoughts.

Father Vincenzo also stopped in frequently. He, too, was a delightful storyteller but Ernesto, the deSicas and David made only short, perfunctional visits and Rita found she did not miss having David stay any longer than the few minutes that he favored her with. His visits were polite and cool and after he would leave she always felt tense and restless. She much preferred Felicianna's visits.

Felicianna's striking beauty enhanced by her warm, considerate manners lifted Rita's spirits more than all the others. She made Rita laugh with her impersonations of some of the more pompous socialites in Urbino. There were many social activities and balls during Festival time and Felicianna had several dressmakers working overtime on her many gowns. It was a mad contest amongst the local women to see who could have the most authentic, historical gown made. Felicianna was estatic on this particular day because a long, lost portrait of her namesake

"Felicianna Larderello" had been found in the bowels of a small museum. It was to be unveiled at the Museum Ball and she, thanks to her Papa's influence, had received secret photographs of this beautiful portrait and was, this very minute, having a copy of the lovely gown made up.

"Isn't it exciting? I shall surely have the most beautiful gown there!" Felicianna clapped gleefully.

Rita smiled back at the vivacious woman, her happiness was so infectious. Rita was glad to be able to share some of that happy feeling.

"But wait. I haven't told you the really good news." Felicianna came to the window where Rita sat in the sun. She took Rita's hands and beaming happily at Rita announced, "Felicianna Lardarella had a lady-in-waiting standing in the background. Her dress, too, is lovely and I am having it made up for you," she squeezed Rita's hands.

"We shall go to the Museum Ball together, you and I, Dante and Carlo," Felicianna spun away, whirling around the room in a mock waltz.

Rita watched the dark, haired, happy woman dance about the room, 'Yes,' she thought 'She's a perfect match for Carlo. So fiery and alive.'

"I'd be happy to be your Lady-in Waiting," Rita answered resignedly. She was deeply moved by the generosity of the young woman moving so gracefully about the room but at the same time she felt a strange loss.

"Wonderful! I'll tell Dante and Carlo. I do hope they will dress. Carlo is such a stick when it comes to costumes." Felicianna waltzed merrily out of the room leaving behind a trace of her earthy perfume to linger in the room, tormenting Rita with visions of Carlo's strong arms holding Felicianna as they whirled around in a sensual, provocative waltz. Rita thought sadly that Felicianna should have no trouble getting Carlo to do her bidding.… for her he would probably dress in sackcloth.

And so the long week passed. Doctor Cuneo finally gave her permission to leave the room. It was with a mixture of joy and anxiety that she entered the dining room that night. To her surprise Dominic Mattini sat on her Aunt Andrea's right. Seating herself on the left, she greeted the somber lawyer.

"I didn't know you were here, Mr. Mattini."

"Carlo drove me up this morning," he answered politely. Then seeing the questioning look in her eyes he continued, "Carlo returned from the States last night and we felt it would be advantageous to drive up together as we had some matters to discuss and I, also, had important business in Perugia which concerned the Molza family."

So that explained why she hadn't had any visits from Carlo this past week. She looked over at the big man sitting across from her and her joy at seeing him again was quickly diminished by the hard, penetrating look he flashed at her, accompanied by a slight nod of his dark head. 'He certainly wasn't showing any enthusiasm at seeing her,' she thought sadly, as she turned to greet the others.

"Now, my dear," interjected Andrea, "Please don't worry your pretty head over any business matters tonight. It's your first night out so, please enjoy the fine meal Sofia has prepared in your honour." Andrea tapped her glass sharply. "Here, here, everyone. A toast to our lovely, Margarita."

They all looked toward Rita raising their glasses. She watched them all. One by one she searched their faces. Could it be one of them that wanted her dead? No, that's crazy. These are friends and relatives. How could I think such a ridiculous thought. She looked at Ernesto, round and jovial, the aloof Kay deSica and her gentle husband, Father Vincenzo, solemn in his black suit, beautiful Felicianna her new friend, especially gay tonight as she sat between Dante and Carlo, then David, fair and rather gaunt looking. She nodded her acknowledgment of the toast, then gave her attention to her artichoke vinargerette. Sofia had indeed prepared a fine meal. The salad was followed by small bowls of creamy Fettucine, noodles swimming in cream, after that a rack of lamb baked with mountain herbs, tiny parselied potatoes, crisp green beans tossed with succulent mushrooms and, of course, two delightful wines. A sweet, sparkling rose and a dryer, white soave bolla. Coffee and tiny pastries full of fresh, whipped cream were served right at the table, as arrangements had been made to attend the Opera in Urbino.

As the dinner group prepared to leave, the cars pulling up to the front door of the Villa, Rita held back. She was suddenly afraid. She realized she was terrified to step out into the open. Waves of fear and nauseasness threatened to bring up her fine dinner. She tried to catch David's attention but he hurried out, head close in conversation with Ernesto. It was a grip of steel that suddenly propelled her towards the door. A deep, husky voice whispered in her ear, "Don't be afraid, Margarita. You don't look half-bad with that shiner." Carlo smiled broadly. Settling her quickly into his small car, leaping around to the driver's side, he folded his long frame in, threw the car in gear and took off towards Urbino.

"Now, that wasn't so bad was it?" he gave her a questioning look. Rita looked back at him gratefully. He seemed so confident, so strong. His big shoulders and thighs threatened to burst the seams of the black tuxedo. His black hair gleamed as he lit a cigarette.

"Smoke?" he held the pack towards her.

"Thanks, I think I will." He handed her his lighter, keeping his eyes on the winding road. Rita lit up and took a long drag. It had been over a week since she'd smoked and the nauseousness and fear mixed with the smoke soon gave her a hacking, dry cough. Quickly, she snuffed out the cigarette. She was coughing so hard tears started down her cheeks and she reached into her evening purse for one of Andrea's lace handkerchiefs. Carlo gave her an amused glance then opened the glove compartment, pulling out a flask.

"Here, drink before you choke to death," he commanded.

Rita gulped a mouthful between coughs, the warm brandy soothed her tortured throat.

"Again," came the harsh command and she drank once more. This time the brandy soothing her enough to stop the coughing. She leaned her head back wearily. Resting quietly for several minutes.

Up ahead, she could see the bright lights of the city of Urbino. Someone in that Festival crowd wanted to kill her. Thugs hired by the unknown Donato Cigno. She suddenly wished she was back in her room at Villa San Giovanni. Safe inside her room with Carlo's burly guard outside the door. She studied Carlo's rugged profile. Yes, it was more than physical power, Carlo gave off an aura of immense inner strength. Oh, how she envied Felicianna. She took another gulp of the brandy, bracing herself for whatever lay ahead. When they pulled up to the entrance of the Opera House, Carlo took the flask from her.

"Are you okay?" he asked.

Rita turned her head away, she just couldn't bear to look into those deep, dark, caring eyes. Something deep inside her was stirring.

He cupped the back of her neck in his big hand, "Margarita, look at me," he pleaded. But just as she was about to turn back to him, the doorman opened the car door and instead she jumped out running to join Andrea, Felicianna and Dante Molza.

For the rest of the evening, Rita never left her seat. She barely heard the wonderful voice of Pavarotti singing "Rigoletto." The entire evening was a blur of faces, voices, and perfumes mixed with the heady scent of masculine after-shaves. She cowered behind Andrea and Father Vincenzo, begging off when Felicianna insisted she join them for some champangne at the intermission. Carlo sat sullenly in a corner of the opera box, coming over to her only when David approached, also begging her to come to the lobby for some Champangne.

"The lady said No," his voice like steel, glaring at David.

"Stay out of this, Molza," David said threateningly.

"I've been in it since the beginning," Carlo shot back.

"It will do you no good," David looked down at the seated Rita. His blue eyes icy, a strange withdrawn expression in them. Rita felt fear wash over her again. She went rigid, her eyes locked on the two men towering over her. She knew instinctively they were not arguing about a glass of champagne. No. This was something far more deadly and she was right in the middle of it all. David stared coldly at her for a brief minute and then turned leaving the opera box abruptly.

The curtain was rising for the last act when Dante and Felicianna returned chatting gaily only to be promptly hushed up by Andrea. Carlo stood behind Rita near the door, whispering to several tuxedo-clad men. "Rigoetto" ended to a standing ovation and Rita was relieved to follow the group out to the waiting cars. Pushing through the crowd in the Lobby with Carlo by her side, she happened to glance over her shoulder at the sea of faces exiting the Opera House. She stopped, puzzled as one of the gentlemen looked vaguely familiar. She looked again, but he was moving away from them towards another Exit. His tall top-hat bobbing and weaving above the crowd. She strained on tip-toe to see him again.

"What is it?" Carlo asked following her gaze.

"Nothing," she answered uneasily, "I thought I recognized a man back there." Carlo turned again. He signaled to another man, who immediately headed in the direction of the weaving top-hat.

The small, red Maserati was in front of them and Carlo quickly settled her in, tipped the doorman and picked his way deftly through the traffic, back up the mountain to Villa san Giovanni. They spoke little. Carlo smoked several cigarettes but Rita wisely declined, earning a mischievious grin from Carlo. Approaching the gate to the Villa, they noticed several cars stopped, their doors wide open. Rita could see men running ahead to where two men scuffled half-way up the embankment. Suddenly, a powerful spot light, illuninated the pair of wrestling men, just as the top-hat was knocked from one of the men's heads. Rita caught a glimpse of red hair. Then the figure was gone, disappearing up the dark, rock strewn hillside. Again, she felt that strange familiarity. She was distracted by the roly-poly figure of Inspectore Adolfo as he approached the car. The Inspectore exchanged several brisk sentences with Carlo in Italian, glancing nervously at Rita time and time again. She yearned to know what they were saying.

"Yes, yes. I understand," nodded Carlo and he pulled around

the parked cars, sped up to the Villa entrance, where he came to a fast stop. He jumped out and ushered Rita into the house before she could even question him.

The fire blazed in the library where the original Opera group had been joined by several others, all strangers to Rita. Carlo's strong hand on her elbow guided her over to the couch where Andrea sat. A tall, very distinguished, gray haired man stood speaking solemnly to Andrea and the others.

"Oh, here they are," she spoke with apparent relief turning towards Carlo and Rita.

"Papa," Carlo warmly kissed the older man on the cheek.

"And, this is Margarita Bondone, I presume," the older man studied Rita, then smiled a warm welcoming smile that lit up his stern face. "You have not had a very joyful welcome home, Margarita, but we shall change that now," he placed a paternal kiss on her cheek.

Rita bristled at the word "home." Her home was in Connecticut, not here in these wild mountains, where strangers killed for unknown reasons.

"Thank you, Mr. Molza," she replied curtly. He ignored her rudness, drawing her aside, he spoke of her Grandfather, her parents and their extensive renovations of Villa Sera.

"What a terrible shame that it was unoccupied for so long a time. Such a beautiful Villa was built for love and laughter, with many bambinos running around," his deep laugh turned Carlo's head as he slouched indolently by the mantle. Rita blushed as their eyes locked, Carlo's black eyes challenging her. The quick exchange did not go unnoticed by Carlo's father who smiled conspiritorily at Andrea.

The evening passed pleasantly enough with only one interuption by Inspectore Adolfo, who spoke privately with Mr. Molza who in turn, with a silent look, sent his two sons, Dante and Carlo on some urgent errand. Rita was awed by the quiet authority Mr. Molza emanated as he sat nonchalantely sipping his brandy.

A modern-day 'Condottiere,' she thought uneasily. And she didn't really relax until Carlo returned to the safety of the library, then she let out a deep sigh of relief. She drank her brandy quickly and the warmth of the liquid relaxed her tense nerves. She wished she could find out what was going on. She tried, but failed in her attempt to join in the social conversation buzzing around her. Her thoughts kept returning to the two men struggling on the embankment. She was greatly relieved when Andrea announced she was retiring and taking Rita along.

"This has been far too much excitment for you on your first day out Come, my dear," she grasped Rita's arm with a trembling hand. The long flight of stairs seemed to leave her exhausted. When Rita kissed the lovely, old woman good-night, she was shocked to see how the last week had aged her Aunt. Worry deeply lined the gentle face and she clung to Rita tightly.

"God bless and keep you, Margarita," she hugged Rita fondly, then disappeared into her room.

Hours later, in her own room, Rita awoke from a troubled sleep. She was shocked to see a dark figure peering out her window. She lay frozen in fear. 'Where was her burly guard?' she glanced over at the door, which was opened a crack, the hall light knifing into the dark bedroom. Should she scream or just make a run for the open door? She looked back at the dark figure, half-turned, the face now visible in the moonlight.

"Carlo," she whispered, sitting up surprised and vastly relieved.

"Sorry, I didn't mean to waken you."

"What are you doing in here?" she demanded.

"Watching for the intruder," he turned back to the window.

Rita shivered, pulling the covers up to her chin, "That man fighting on the embankment?" she asked.

"Yes, your dear cousin."

"My COUSIN?" Rita asked incredously. That flash of red hair when the top-hat fell off. Oh, Yes. She started to rise from the bed, shocked and stunned.

"Paul O'Neil? Cousin Paul?"

Carlo strode swiftly to her, grasping her bare shoulders he looked deep into her shocked eyes. "Margarita, he's in on this. He wants you out of the way."

"No, it can't be. Why? Why? The Villa? Does he want the Villa? He can have it. I don't want it. I hate it. Do you hear me? I hate that Villa. I never wanted it. Paul can have it, do you understand me?" her voice had risen and she began hitting Carlo with her clenched fists, over and over on his broad chest. He grabbed her wrists, pulling her arms down behind her.

"It's alright, Bruno. I'll handle this," he spoke to the burly guard, who hearing the commotion had stepped into the room. The big man nodded silently, stepping back out.

"Relax, Margarita. It's not the Villa, Paul wants. It's what he thinks is buried there." Carlo pulled her close, kissing her lightly on the forehead. "The Duchess Taranta's jewels."

"You mean those jewels I read about in the history books? There really are such jewels?"

"The very same," he grinned at her, "Your parents actually uncovered them when they renovated the Villa." He released her wrists only to encase her buttocks in his big hands. His dark eyes devoured her slim figure in the revealing, white nightgown. She felt the heat of his hands and she attempted to bring her arms up between their close bodies but he was too swift. Drawing her soft white body up against his hard, muscular one. He kissed her firmly on the lips.

Still in shock over the news of Paul O'Neil, Rita passively enjoyed the kiss, which slowly turned into a more passionate, demanding one. She realized, suddenly, that her cold fear had been replaced by a hot fire racing through her half-naked body. She was pressing, achingly into Carlo's firm, hard body. The sweet, passive kiss had become a tangle of wet, probing tongues. Her white arms circled his broad shoulders, pale against his black tuxedo. His hot hands pressed her lower body forcefully against his own throbbing body and she responded by tightening her hold on the massive back. She ached to draw him ever closer, tighter. Slowly, he lifted her back onto the bed kissing her neck, her bare shoulders. Pressing down on her until they lay side by side. Carlo gently drew down the strap of her nightgown, his strong hand feather-light on her white skin. He brushed his fingers across her bare breast.

"You are so beautiful, my Margarita," his searing lips played with her aroused nipple, finally taking it completely in his warm mouth. Rita thought she would faint from joy. Tremors of sheer passion rocked her shaking body. Never had she felt so on fire. Carlo had discovered a hidden volcano within her that threatened to erupt. He stopped kissing her breast, raising his head, he looked into her loving eyes.

"Now, I can hold you, forever. No one shall ever tear us apart again," he whispered solemnly, then kissed her fiercely, his passion overpowering him. He roughly ripped aside her fragile, white night-gown and she lay completely naked beneath his hot, caressing hands. They roamed over her trembling body, causing sensations she never dreamed of. She eagerly kissed his mouth, his eyes, his ears. She nibbled on his thick neck while his warm fingers flickered lightly over her breasts, down across her taunt stomach, along the inside of her slightly, parted thighs.

"Oh, Carlo, I love you," the words escaped her fevered lips.

He drew his hand slowly away and she arched her pelvis silently begging him not to stop. He pressed gently on her stomach, then upwards to cup her throbbing breast. Running his lips along her neck, his tongue sending shivers of delight throughout her body. She tried to reach inside the ruffled shirt, yearning to feel the touch of his bare skin against her own. He sat up and quickly removed the shirt and she caressed his broad, back with it's tense muscles. He stood to remove the awkward suspenders and cumberband, cursing the 'damn tux', and as he turned, still in his black pants, she could see the thickness, the readiness of him. Carlo stared intently at the opened door. The shadow of the burly guard fell across the hall carpet.

"Shit," Carlo snarled, throwing the balled up shirt into a corner. He looked down at Rita, drinking in her lovely, naked body with his hungry eyes. Suddenly, he snapped the coverlet over her, stormed over to the windows and lit a cigarette. Rita watched him furiously puffing on the cigarette, the moon-light playing on his naked upper body. She could see the dark, curly hairs on his wide chest, see the muscles in his arms, his big, wide shoulders. She longed to have him back beside her. Lying close, his warm naked body full length alongside her.

"Carlo," she called softly.

"Go to sleep," he snapped coldy. Rita was stunned. She felt as if ice water had been thrown over her. She shrunk beneath the coverlet. Tears brimmed her eyes, her legs started trembling, and soon her entire body was shaking. She felt so humiliated. She wasn't even woman enough for him to finish what he had started. She sobbed aloud, unable to control her tears. She saw Carlo start back towards the bed and she quickly rolled over, turning her back on him and burying her face into the pillow.

'That beast. That animal. I'll never let him hear me cry!' she vowed, struggling to control her wounded emotions. She lay stiff and quiet. Choking back her sobs as the tears streamed down her face. Why had she allowed herself to be so easily swayed by Carlo's charm? Why would he want her when he had Felicianna? Why did she melt so quickly every time he kissed her? Damn him! He had been toying with her, that's all. God, how I hate him~!

Rita finally fell into an exhausted, haunted sleep, where once again as a young girl, she ran screaming up the twisting, mountain path only to be caught and held by strong arms. The dream was especially vivid this time and she saw that she didn't struggle against the strong arms holding her so firmly, no, she seemed to relax in the strong arms and in doing so she slept easier afterwards.

Chapter 11

At breakfast, Rita was relieved to find Carlo missing from the table. The ever talkative Ernesto informed her that along with Dante and Felicianna he had driven back to Urbino to pick up the ball-gowns for this evening's Museum Ball. Carlo's father was seated next to Andrea, both looking rather grim, when she sat down to help herself to a cup of coffee.

"Margarita, I'm sorry to have to tell you that the Polizia appreheded the man who shot at you the other day," said the grim gray-haired man.

"Sorry, Why sorry? I'm thrilled to hear such good news."

"Margarita, it was Paul. Cousin Paul," Andrea replied tightly, dabbing at her eyes with her lace handkerchief.

Ernesto and the deSicas and the others all gasped and started to talk amongst themselves about this startling news. Rita picked at her breakfast, she felt an overwhelming sadness.

Mario Molza seeing her distress, tried to lighten the blow. "When questioned by Inspectore Adolfo, your cousin readily admitted firing the high-powered rifle found in his car. But he insisted he was only trying to warn you. He said he had tried to frighten you from coming to Urbino by calling you at your hotel in Rome." Rita simply didn't want to believe the soft-spoken Mr. Molza. Her own cousin! Why they had grown up together. She gazed dumbstruck while he continued to explain Paul's tenuous ties to the terrorist group, Tre-Scalini. It seems that while in Rome, he lived with a young woman identified as "Margo" who was a long standing member of the Tre-Scalini. Having learned from Paul that he was next in line to inherit the Villa Sera, she passed this information on to the terrorists and they sent the men in the black Alfeta to 'arrange' an accident for you." He put his big, warm hand over her cold, trembling one, as she sat in stunned disbelief. Rita looked up into his dark concerned eyes. So much like Carlo's. She felt her own eyes beginning to fill with unshed tears.

"Margarita, your father was my dearest friend. Our families go back for generations. I give you my solemn vow that this strange mystery will be cleared up quickly," he squeezed her hand encouragingly. Rita could only nod silently, afraid if she spoke the dam would break. All the tears she had refused to shed for her parents, her handsome fiancée, her weak, suicidal namesake, Aunt Margarita, the mother of the very man who had tried to kill her. All these well-up tears were now ready to fall for a mixed-up red-haired, quasi-terrorist, who had turned on his own cousin. Playmate of his childhood. Rita wanted to laugh and cry at the same time. Why was it so sad? She had never escaped the past! She had only deceived herself momentarily. This was her true legacy, this evil Bondone curse. Was she never to be free? She gulped some coffee, took a bite of dry toast and finding it almost impossible to swallow, stood and excused herself, walking to the far end of the terrace.

Rita felt empty and lost. The thought of the Bondone curse haunted her and she wanted to leave these mountains and all this violence. She thought of Louisa-Maria's lonely existence back in Boston. The tragic loss of her husband and child in the terrible fire. Now, Paul again the cause of more horror. What a tortured soul he must be! She glanced down at the rooftop of Villa Sera, the sunlight flashing off the blue, tiled roof. She stepped off the terrace onto a graveled path bordered in red geraniums. She strolled along following the winding path through the garden, her mind wandering over the years. Was she finally being forced to face reality? Could all these tragedies be the result of the Bondone curse, passed from generation to generation? If she could sell the Villa Sera, go back to Connecticut and marry David, could she escape the curse? If she cut all her ties with Urbino, would she and her future children be safe from the Bondone Curse? A picture of Carlo's broad, naked back, illuminated by the moon-light the other night intruded into her thoughts of David and Connecticut.

"No," she plucked a red geranium, twisting it over and over,

"It's not fair!" she railed, "I had nothing to do with that past history," she angrily ripped petals from the blossom letting them shift through her fingers. Watching the petals, she became aware of the view below her. She could see some of the Fountain of the Tortoises.

"Why there must be another way into the garden at Villa Sera," she spoke aloud, surprised at this new discovery. Looking around, all she saw was dense mountain undergrowth broken by tall cypress trees. Walking further along the path, she came to a high rododendrum bush, which rose seven or more feet in the air. She noticed a slight clearing behind the colorful bush. By carefully pushing aside one long, heavily laden branch, she was able to step inside the bush.

Several feet in front of her she could see a narrow opening in the mountain undergrowth. Leaving her flowery archway behind, she started down the narrow, overgrown path. In minutes she was standing before the Fountain of the Tortoises. She glanced nervously at the stone bench afraid she might see two hooded figures seated there. But, no, the garden was empty, tranquil and rosy in the morning sunlight. Flowers struggled to live amongst the overgrown weeds. The blue, mosaic tile lay in neat rows free from any stain of blood. Rita ran her hands over the marble fountain. How she had loved to come here with her Mother. She would read her school lessons while Mama painted at her easel. The fountain gurgling and splashing as the water spouted from the Dolphin's mouth and the little cherubs heads tucked under the big, upper bowl. Rita reached up playfully patting the tortoise, each tortoise squirmed differently in it's valient effort to reach the water above, held precariously in the faun-boy's outstretched hand. She moved on to the next tortoise, grabbing it's scally hind-leg which protruded at on odd angle. She was surprised when it moved at her touch.

"Well," she thought, feeling it move again, "that will have to be fixed before it falls off and smashes." She climbed into the lower bowl to get a closer look.

"What ever am I doing?" she caught herself, exasperated.

"I'm selling this Villa, what do I care about a loose tortoise," she started to step back down, then stopped. Her dream flashed before her….the image of the faun-boy holding something out to her. She stared up at the tortoise, comic in its struggle to get back in the upper bowl and find water, it's scaly hind-legs kicking away. Her fingers grasped one of the scaly legs, then the other and she gave a hard pull. She screamed as she fell backwards, landing painfully on the hard blue tile. Rita looked down at her lap in shock where the playful tortoise lay. On close examination she found it was not made of mable like the rest of the fountain, instead heavy iron, she guessed. Turning it over, she discovered tiny hinges on the inside perimeter of the tortoise shell. She tried to pull it open but was unsuccessfull.

"Well, little fellow, I guess you're going up to Villa San Giovanni until I can get you open." Rita rose tucking the tortoise under her arm, she headed back up the hidden path.

She had just rounded the first bend after emerging from the rhododendum bush when she ran head-long into the deSicas.

"Well, hello, there," Greg deSica seemed genuinely surprised, while Kay looked sharply at Rita, making a mental note of the tortoise tucked under Rita's arm.

"Hello Greg, hello Kay. There are some gorgeous flowers along this path. Enjoy your walk," Rita smiled too brightly, stepping around them quickly, she hurried on. She wanted the privacy of her room so she could pry open the tortoise. She was frightened at the thought that she was sure she knew what was in the playful tortoise. She hurried across the terrace, praying she wouldn't meet anyone else. She scampered up to her room.

Once inside, her suspicions were confirmed. Her bed sparkled with brilliant white diamonds, flashing green emeralds, deep blood, red rubies, and smooth, creamy pearls lay mingled with pieces of icy silver and warm gold. Rita allowed the letter opener to fall from her lifeless fingers to the carpet. She was mesmerized by the gleaming treasures before her. She knelt beside the bed picking up a beautiful, square, emerald brooch, turning it around and around, fascinated by it's cold beauty. Rita stared into its depths where she saw the sweet face of the murdered young boy whose mother had refused to ever wear these jewels again. She dropped the emerald, recoiling in horror.

'Oh, yes,' she thought sadly, 'some WOULD kill for such beauties.'

With that, she jumped to her feet. Frantically, she began

scooping the jewels back into the tortoise. Hating the touch of the cold gems. She wished she had never found them. She started to sob, "I must get rid of them." Then she heard footsteps coming down the hall. The tortoise was awkward and heavy as she held it to her shaking breast, searching the room with her terrified eyes for a hiding spot. A sharp rap on the door made Rita cringe in terror. Clutching the tortoise tighter to her breast she watched in fascinated horror as the doorknob turned. She held her breath, praying that whoever it was would go away. After what seemed like an eternity, she heard the person turn and walk back down the hall.

Rita collapsed on the edge of the bed, her knees shaking. Her head began to throb and the vision in her right eye began to blur. In a daze she thrust the tortoise under her bed, happy to be rid of it. Standing, she remarked out loud, "After lunch, you are going right back where you came from." Locking the door securely behind her, she started down the hall to lunch.

Chapter 12

The terrace was bright with tubs of yellow and white tulips. The blue umbrellas replaced with green and white striped ones. Felicianna stood out in her halter dress of sea-foam green. Dante and Carlo handsome in white pants, Dante in a dark green shirt, Carlo's all white.

"Oh, here she is," exclaimed Felicianna as Rita walked towards them. Carlo turned his penetrating eyes raking her body. Rita felt sure he could see right through her lilac blouse and skirt. She tossed him a defiant look. She had made up her mind the minute she had seen him sitting under the umbrella, that he was not going to get the best of her this time. She would not be toyed with again! She turned her attention to Dante and Felicianna.

After his curt hello, Carlo had sunk into a black mood, drinking heavily of the luncheon wine. And just to spite him, Rita flirted with Dante, who responded eagerly. She found him much more talkative than the intense Carlo. As the lunch happily progressed, Dante soon made her forget the dangerous errand she still had to complete that afternoon. Rita was so engrossed with flirting with Dante, to spite Carlo for the previous evenings humiliation, she never noticed the smile fade from Felicianna's bright lips. But she did notice when Carlo leaned towards Felicianna, putting his long arm around her, resting his big hand on her bare shoulder. He whispered something in her ear and Felicianna smiled weakly, nervously twirling the stem of her wine glass. Again, Carlo whispered in her ear. Rita felt her stomach tighten and she ached with jealousy. She longed to throw her wine in Carlo's handsome face. Instead, she turned to Dante and deliberately leaned closer pressing her breast against his arm. Dante said something to her but she never heard him because she was watching Carlo tilt Felicianna's chin up, look into her dark eyes, then stand quickly.

"If you two love-birds don't mind, we are leaving," Carlo pulled Felicianna roughly to her feet. His dark eyes blazed at Rita. She glared back at him. Finally, pulling her eyes away from Carlo, her eyes met Felicianna'a and she was shocked at the look of pure hatred blazing back at her. Dante spoke sharply to Felicianna in Italian and she gasped, hurrying away from the table.

"You bastard!" Carlo clenched his fists. But Dante just laughed heartily and put his arm around Rita, pulling her close. Carlo opened and closed his fists, rocking back on his heels, he towered over them menacingly. Dante laughed insolently at his younger brother.

"Be careful, Dante. You won't get away with it this time, you rotten bastard!" Carlo growled then hurried after Felicianna.

Rita's flirtation with Dante was halted by the arrival of Father Vincenzo and David, who joined them at the table.

Father Vincenzo had been keeping David busy visiting all the beautiful churches and art museums here in the Marches. As the three men talked of history and art, Rita sat pondering how little she had seen of David. Soon they would be returning to the States. But she sensed that their relationship had changed. It had never been a passionate one. She had never experienced that deep longing to come together as one with David. Oh, yes, she admitted. She had wanted to experience sex with David, wanted to know what it was all about. How it felt. To really just get it over with. Rather a clinical attitude, she thought bitterly. Now, after last night, she worried if she could really arouse any man to fulfillment. Carlo certainly had cooled off quickly. Rita looked down at her slim body. "What's wrong with me?" she wondered sadly. "Did I look like a flat schoolgirl laying there naked? Was there something I should have done that I didn't do?" She could picture Carlo's big hand on Felicianna's bare shoulder, her heavy breasts bursting out of her green, halter-dress. Frustrated and jealous, Rita drank more wine than she should have. She caught Father Vincenzo watching her closely.

"Excuse me," she interrupted "I think I'll go to my room and take a nap. I want to be up to tonight's Ball," she hurried away, not caring about David's startled look, nor Dante's strange one.

She did sleep for an hour awakening with a start. Remembering her dangerous errand, she checked out the window that the terrace was clear of luncheon guests, then picked up the tortoise and stole quietly down the stairs. She gave a prayer of thanks that the burly guards had been removed after Paul O'Neil's arrest. Dashing across the empty Terrace, she bolted down the main path. 'No time for long, garden strolls,' she thought, thinking of the other secret path. The Tortoise was heavy in her arms and she slipped twice on the rock, strewn path. She raced madly down, eager to be rid of the deadly jewels.

The sun was lower now, giving the garden at Villa Sera a gray, ominous look. Shadows stretched long, dark fingers here and there. Rita stood for a moment shivering in the archway. She was hesitant to enter the shadowy garden. Bracing herself, she dashed to the fountain. Scrambling up into the lower bowl, she tried to fit the heavy tortoise back up in position but it kept sliding back down. Desperate to finish her task and be away from the gloomy garden, Rita placed her foot on the boy-faun's out-stretched knee and hoisted herself up higher. She placed the tortoise's front legs into the upper bowl balancing the scaly tail on the boy-faun's upraised fingers. The tortoise hung precariously for a second and then settled in place. Rita jumped down, surveying the fountain. Satisfied her replaced tortoise looked the same as the others, she turned to leave.

"Beautiful isn't it?" Dante Molza stood in the archway. "You had me worried, honey," he came to her and put his arms around her.

"I thought you would never come out. What took you so long?" he kissed her neck.

"What ARE you talking about?" Rita tried to break away from his strong grasp.

"You know what I'm talking about, Baby." he cupped her breast and pressed a hot, wet kiss on her lips.

"Wait a minute, Dante." She struggled away from his persistent kisses, pushing on his arms trying to disengage herself from his strong hold. Rita soon found she was no match for the muscular Dante and she felt herself being slowly lowered to the cold blue tiles.

"Dante, please, for God's Sake, what are you doing?" she asked him frantically. But he wasn't to be stopped by her verbal protests.

As soon as he had her down, his hand was up her skirt, caressing her bare thigh.

"No!" she screamed, frightened into action, she pushed at him while pulling down her skirt at the same time. "Let me go Dante!" she demanded.

"Don't be silly, Baby. You know you want it as much as I do," he kissed her again, squeezing her roughly on the breast.

"Stop it, you are hurting me." Rita rolled her body away. Scratching at his hand cupping her breast.

"Ouch! You little wild cat. So that's how you like it. Well, Baby I can play that game!" and he slapped her hard across the face.

Bright lights shot through her head, then sharp stabbing pain. Her vision on the right failed completely. She felt nauseaus, bile bubbled up in her throat, then miraculously, she felt Dante's weight being lifted off her. She heard voices shouting and she peered into the shadows to see Carlo and Dante fighting fiercely. Carlo punched Dante again and again. Rita heard bone crack, she saw blood pour out of Dante's nose. The garden was much darker now and thicker, blacker shadows shut out most of the filtering, fading light.

"Heaven help me," she pleaded to the darkness. She thought she was going crazy. Carlo and Dante struggling in the dark garden brought back all the horror of her nightmare. She wanted to be away from this evil place.

"Carlo. Carlo. Please," she cried out to him to stop. Finally, he threw his brother down.

"I should have done that years ago, you bastard!" he spat in disgust at Dante. Then sweeping Rita into his arms, he carried her up the mountain path back to her room. Placing her gently on the bed, he got some cold water and made her swallow some aspirins. She looked up at him towering over her, his eyes questioning her silently.

"I did not go there to meet Dante," she explained.

"No?" he said flatly.

"No! He must have followed me," she said emphatically.

"Well, what did you expect? You threw yourself at him at lunch," Carlo retorted angrily.

Rita looked helplessly up at him, she had to admit he was right again. She couldn't deny that she had flirted, had teased Dante.

"This isn't Connecticut, sweetheart," Carlo snapped, his eyes blazing with fury. He turned on her and strode from the room. Rita rolled over, sobs racking her bruised body.

"Damn him! Damn all the Molzas," she cried.

Chapter 13

Later a wave of hopelessness filled Rita as Felicianna swept into the room, followed by Sofia. Their arms loaded down with the plastic-covered ballgown and petticoats. Rita stood in her navy terri-cloth bathrobe, having showered and shampooed her short, blond hair, which she rubbed briskly with a dry towel.

"Aunt Andrea thought you might need some assistance putting on your ballgown. Heaven knows, you Americans rarely dress," Felicianna announced icily, sweeping over to fuss with her own dark hair in front of the mirror. Rita stared at the dark-haired woman in her off-the-shoulder gown of ruby velvet, which accented the full bosom, and showed off her lovely, pale shoulders.

Rita felt completely inadequate as she watched Felicianna, 'She's so womanly, so feminine,' she thought miserably as she caught a whiff of Felicianna's strong, earthy perfume.

"Well, hurry up! Don't stand there gawking like a country bumpkin!" Felicianna whirled around ripping off the plastic covers from Rita's gown. Sofia gave Felicianna a nasty look and huffed out of the room but, first, giving Rita a kindly pat on the shoulder.

Rita dreaded dressing in front of Felicianna, she felt just like the awkward, country bumpkin Felicianna thought her to be.

She turned her back on the beautiful, dark haired woman and quickly slipped into the under-garments Sofia had laid out on the chair.

"You certainly ARE thin," observed Felicianna "I hope the gown will fit properly. You haven't ANY hips at all!" she snapped.

Rita smoothed the petticoat over her boyish hips and turned to face Felicianna. She wanted to run and scratch the beautiful face studying her with such hostile eyes.

"Well, there it is." Felicianna waved at the bed where a lovely gown of pale, blue satin lay. "I hope you can do it justice." She whirled back to the mirror.

Rita's heart sank. She trembled as she lifted the lovely, soft gown, slipping it over her head. She thought she would be nauseous again, as the sharp pains began stabbing in her head. She sat on the edge of the bed, pressing her right eye. She prayed for the pain to leave.

"What's wrong?" Felicianna asked watching her in the mirror.

"Nothing." Rita lied as she rose unsteadily and went over to the mirror. The image that looked back at her was of a petite blond, swathed in a blue satiny haze.

"What has happened to your eye?" the other girl asked.

Rita looked closer and discovered that her right cheek just below her eye was turning black and blue again.

"Oh, no," she said hopelessly. "Damn that Dante!"

"Dante?" Felicianna went chalk white. "Dante did that to you?" she grasped Rita's arms, searching Rita's face for an answer. Rita pulled away from her hold.

"Yes, he did. But it was all a misunderstanding."

"All? What ALL? What else happened?" Felicianna looked ready to faint. Rita looked at her puzzled.

"I said it was nothing!" she replied annoyed. Why should Felicianna care what Dante did when she had Carlo at her beck and call.

"Oh, no. Not again. He couldn't," Felicianna threw herself onto the bed and burst into sobs. Stunned Rita sat beside her patting her heaving back.

"Nothing happened, Felicianna. Believe me. Dante misunderstood my actions at lunch. He just came on a bit strong that's all." Rita minimized the ugly scene in the garden for the sake of the sobbing girl, although she still didn't understand why that seemed to be necessary.

"Besides, what do you care what Dante does, you are in love with Carlo," Rita added. Felicianna's head shot up and she glared at Rita.

"Love Carlo? You fool. You stupid foolish woman. I LOVE Dante. Dante! Do you hear?" she hissed like a wildcat at Rita, whose mouth dropped open in amazement.

"But, I thought you and Carlo…." she trailed off foolishly.

"Carlo is my friend. My dearest friend. And I do love him but not the way you think." Felicianna dabbed her wet eyes with a corner of the coverlet. She looked at Rita, pity and pain mixed in her dark eyes.

"Oh, Margarita, I'm so sorry," she touched Rita's cheek gently.

"Dante can't help himself. He gets carried away and then can't stop," she began sobbing again and lay back down on the pillows.

Rita was deeply moved. She had never heard anyone cry so soulfully.

"Please, Felicianna don't cry. I really don't want Dante. I never really did. I only flirted with him to make Carlo jealous."

"You love Carlo?" Felicianna asked, stopping her pitiful crying to sit up and stare at Rita.

"Yes, no, I mean I guess so," Rita answered, unsure of her true feelings for the handsome Carlo.

"Oh, how wonderful!" Felicanna threw her arms around Rita. "Now we can be friends again. Even better, maybe, sisters-in-law, if only…" her voice trailed off sadly.

"Margarita, I must tell you. I must talk to a woman," she wrung her hands together "all these years, I've had only Carlo to talk to. I have been so ashamed." Felicianna searched Rita's face with her tear-filled eyes. Slowly she began talking, choosing her words carefully at first, then in a torrent of pent-up agony revealing her wretched secret to Rita.

"You see, I love Dante. I have always loved him, since we were both small children. I was just sixteen and Dante was home from the University for the summer. It was a warm night, and I loved him so, I just didn't have the willpower to refuse him," she looked into Rita's eyes pleading for understanding. Rita nodded, remembering her own pleas for Carlo to return to the very same bed they now sat on. 'Oh, those damn Molzas!' Rita thought bitterly. She could picture the young Felicianna succumbing to the ardent advances of the strong Dante. Rita felt tears running down her cheeks, as the dark-haired beauty told of finding herself pregnant and Dante leaving to return to the University and she too terrified to tell her parents had turned to Dante's younger brother, Carlo. He, in turn, had rushed out driving immediately to Rome to see Dante at school. When Carlo returned, ashen-faced to tell Felicianna that he, himself, would marry her. She knew, Dante had refused her, cast her aside like some "puttanta"—whore. She had declined Carlo's kind offer of marriage and then, run like a madwoman out into the night, flinging herself off the steep mountainside. Rita gasped as the picture of the beautiful, young girl falling, crashing, down the rock-strewn mountain filled her mind.

It was Carlo who organized the torch-light search party and it was, he, who found her broken and barely breathing at the bottom of a deep crevice. She had lost the baby and spent the next four years learning to walk again.

"But for God's mercy and Carlo's loving encouragement, I would be a cripple today," Felicianna concluded.

"But how can you still love Dante?" Rita asked incredulously.

Felicianna shrugged resignedly, "For some women there is only one man. Dante is my first and only man. Can you understand that, Margarita?"

Rita stared back at her new friend, she thought of David and her dead fiancé and Carlo. Carlo made her feel as none of the others had.

"Yes, maybe, I can understand," she murmured.

"Oh, thank you, Margarita." Felicianna kissed Rita warmly on both cheeks. "It's so wonderful to have a girlfriend to talk to."

They laughed and hugged each other.

"Good Heavens, look at us," Felicianna exclaimed, leaping to her feet and brushing the wrinkles from her ruby gown. "Come, we must freshen up." She pulled Rita to her feet and the two girls rushed to repair their tear-stained faces.

The Museum Ball was in full swing when their party arrived. There were two large ballrooms, each with it's own Orchestra playing lively dance tunes. Candelabra's blazed amidst masses of greenery and flowers of every color, size and species. Rita's attention was immediately drawn to the right of the main ballroom entrance where white orchids seemed to float etherally in a sea of bright red geraniums. She raised her eyes to the mirror above and was suddenly reminded of her dream. She shook her head to clear it.

Not tonight. She was determined to have a good time. She caught her breath as she saw David approaching behind her. Whirling around she held out her arms.

"David, you DO look grand." He was, indeed, handsome in his dark, green velvet suit with a cream ascot pinned at the throat with a large mother-of-pearl stickpin.

"Thank you, Rita," he kissed her lightly on the cheek. "But I should be complimenting you, for you must be the most lovely woman here tonight," he held her at arms length. "You are a vision from Heaven. Swarthed in your sky-blue gown."

Rita laughed merrily. She meant to enjoy tonight. She felt herself relaxing, the tension created by her falling out with Felicianna over her foolish flirtation with Dante, was completely dispelled. She was happy they were friends again.

She and David strolled into the main ballroom arm in arm. Rita smiled at Felicanna in Dante's arms, as the two whirled around the dance floor. Dante's nose looked flat and there were ugly bruises appearing on his swollen chin.

"Poor man, had a bad auto accident only this very afternoon." Father Vincenzo had announced solemnly at cocktails.

Rita realized she would never fully understand how Felicianna could still love Dante after the miserable way he had treated her. But she was secretly relieved that Felicianna did not love Carlo. But she, then, asked herself, 'Why should that matter?' She forced herself to stop searching the crowded ballroom for a glimpse of the tall, dark-haired man.

"What possible difference does it make anyway?" and she pressed closer to David as they danced around the beautiful, marble-pillared ballroom. The orchestra began playing "Through the Years" and Rita couldn't help but think back on that fateful, moonlit, night on the mountain. Her own father had struck and killed a man on that terrible moonlit night. Somehow she knew the struggle started over the jewels and she was glad she had replaced the jewels in their secret, hiding place. She never wanted to see them again. Nothing had ever been the same after that night. She shuddered, stepping on David's toe.

"What is it, Rita?" David asked, "Shall we sit and have a drink?"

"Yes, maybe that's what I need," she readily agreed finding it was becoming difficult to concentrate on their dancing. David seemed glad to sit down. He ordered their drinks and when they arrived handed Rita hers and stood with his in his hand, looking out over the crowd.

"So, tomorrow you'll be through here. Mattini has the papers all ready?" David asked bluntly.

"Why, yes," Rita answered perplexed. She looked up at David, who stood studying the passing dancers, a closed look on his face. She sat, twisting her glass. It was the first time David had directly inquired about any of the Villa business. She supposed he was anxious to get back to the States. It was just so strange, when she could have used some of his expert advice a few days back, he was nowhere to be found. She studied David's face. He was not enjoying himself, she could tell. He seemed tense, his eyes traveled about the ballroom never stopping but probing every corner.

Rita sipped her drink. Did David suspect something between Carlo and her. She sincerely hoped not but something was different about David tonight. He's changed since we've been in Urbino, she thought. His tall, blond, good looks drew many admiring glances from the beautiful women being whirled around the dance floor. David stood, feet apart, hands clasped behind his back, the dark green suit contrasting sharply with his light, sandy hair. His long, lean legs were flexed, ready for action.

"David," Rita spoke hesitantly, wanting to clear whatever had clouded their relationship. She rose from her chair, meaning to speak quietly with him but David turned sharply, shocking Rita with a piercing, contemptuous look. A cold chill ran through her but was quickly dispersed by David's boyish grim.

"They give quite a party up here, don't they?" he remarked, his grin not quite covering up for the sarcastic tone in his cool voice.

As Rita searched for her voice to answer, they were joined by Andrea, looking stately in her long, black gown and Father Vincenzo somber in his black suit. The talk turned to the rivalry among the Marches, mountain families and their centuries-old desire to out-wit, to out-smart each other. Father Vincenzo again entertaining them with hilarious tales of thwarted political and romantic plans.

Their small group swelled as Ernesto Feltre, escorting a stout but pleasant, gray-haired woman, and another couple joined them. After introductions, Ernesto's friend asked Rita to dance. He was a smooth accomplished dancer and they had a lively turn around the crowded, floor. Returning to the table, Rita was disturbed and pleased to see Carlo sitting next to her empty chair. There was no way she could politely escape him so she sat demurely down, thanking Ernesto's friend for the dance.

"You look beautiful tonight," Carlo spoke low and huskily. Staring at the soft, swelling of her pale breasts above the blue satin of her tight bodice.

Rita felt herself blushing, wishing that he would look elsewhere. "I hope you didn't hurt your hand too much," she nodded at his bruised right hand. The knuckles were scraped and swollen. But small damage compared to what he had inflicted on Dante's face.

"It's fine," he flexed his long fingers, opening and closing his huge hand in a tight fist. "And how is the 'damsel in distress' this evening? No serious after effects, I hope?" he smiled, his dark eyes warm and questioning.

"I'm fine, also, Carlo. I want to apologize. I...I..." she stammered, then rushed on "Well, I had a long talk with Felicianna this afternoon and she told me all about her and Dante."

Carlo's eyes widened in surprise and Rita hurried on "I'm really sorry I acted like such a fool at lunch. I have come to love Felicianna like a sister and I would never, knowingly, do anything to hurt her." She looked apologetically at Carlo. He put his big, bruised hand over Rita's nervous, twitching ones. The warmth of his touch sending waves of longing through her tense, stiff body.

"Margarita, sweetheart, you are so naïve," the dark eyes were piercing in their intensity, his touch on her hand so firm. She felt she was drowning in his embracing stare. She struggled back.

"I am not naïve," she retaliated. She hated his tone of voice. And she resented his treating her like a child.

"Well, then, you THINK like a dumb kid. What the hell did you expect from Dante after rubbing yourself all over him?" Carlo removed his hand to take a long drink from his tall glass.

Rita was furious, "I did not rub myself all over Dante," she enunciated each word coldly. She wondered why they always ended up arguing, as she stared back at Carlo with icy, blue eyes.

"No matter, now. I think I've straightened out Dante," he stated confidently, "But you, that's another problem altogether. Come on, let's dance," and he pulled her onto the dance floor.

Rita intended to punish him for his insulting remarks by being cool and aloof. She looked icily into his relaxed, handsome face. He ignored her cold look with a flicker of an amused smile, and pressed his strong body close to her. His warm breath caressed the tip of her ear. She was, suddenly overcome by a desperate need to reach up and kiss his firm, full lips. The Scotch she had drunk too fast began to make her woozy. She missed a step.

"I'm sorry, I guess I'm getting a little dizzy, what with the crowd and all the excitement," she certainly didn't want him thinking he had any effect on her.

"I see," he said smugly "Well, a little air should clear your head, my sweet Blue Angel," and he whirled her through the marble columns out onto the terrace.

The air was brisk and glittering stars crowned the twin mountain peaks. A full moon cast a silvery glow over the valley far below them as they stood at the balustrade. They both breathed deep, long breaths, then turned, laughing towards each other.

Rita spoke first, "It's really so lovely up here in the mountains." 'Sometimes.' She added, mentally, to herself.

"Yes, I have always loved it here. I'm rather glad I was called back." Carlo's eyes drank in the magnificent panorama of stars and mountains.

"Called back?" Rita asked puzzled.

"Yes, Father insisted that I return this summer. There was some unfinished business that had to be 'attended to," he looked down pensively at Rita's small, oval face. Cupping it in his huge hands, he kissed her gently on the lips.

"But I don't understand, Carlo." She tried to think as his warm lips traveled up to her bruised cheek, barely visible under her make-up, he softly kissed the tender spot, then kissed her eyes, her forehead and back down to her bare neck and shoulders. "But…but I thought you lived here in Urbino," she pulled away wanting some answers before she melted completely under his warm lips.

"Whatever gave you that idea? I left the Marches years ago, but not because I was ashamed of my heritage like you. I've been a lawyer in Los Angeles for several years. We have extensive holdings in California," he studied her curiously.

Rita was stunned. She couldn't believe she had been so wrong about Carlo. "But you…" she sputtered, "You are so…"

"I'm so what?" it was his turn to be puzzled now by Rita's confused state of mind. Grasping her shoulders he held her away from his tall body, waiting for her to continue.

"Well, you are so old-fashioned," she sputtered out. "You are still so…so…Old World, so to speak."

Carlo stiffened, his grip on her shoulders became much tighter: "That bothers you?" when she didn't answer he shook her by the shoulders, his fingers cutting through the soft, satin to hurt her.

"Yes. No. I mean, oh Carlo, I don't know what I mean." she was hurt and frightened at the sudden change in him. Gone was the tender warmth, replaced by a cold, penetrating stare.

"You are some kind of girl. I never would have believed that you would turn out like this. You Dad was so proud of you. You were his "Golden Girl." I don't understand you, Rita. You think I'm "Old World" because I come back when my Father needs me? You think I'm old fashioned because I worry about some blond nut that runs around lonely mountain roads half-naked? Well, do you?" he shook her again much more roughly.

Rita cowered at the black fury in his dark eyes. His jaw muscles jumped in his taut face, she couldn't answer him, her mouth was so dry. Tears came to her eyes as the pain in her shoulders spread down her back. He pulled her roughly to him, kissing her hard, forcing her lips apart, penetrating her dry mouth with his hot, wet tongue. His big hand grabbed the back of her blond head, pushing savagely he forced her closer and closer, pressing ever harder on her soft lips with his hot, hard mouth. His long tongue probing and pushing until finally gagging her. Then he thrust her away, turning indifferently to light a cigarette.

"Isn't that what you modern, liberated women like?" he snarled.

Rita stood with a shaking hand covering her bruised lips. She recoiled in horror from the harsh, brutal man who stood casually smoking a few feet from her. She had been a fool to even consider Carlo on the same plane as David. They were worlds; apart.

"You beast! You're just like your brother, you and Dante. You are cut from the same cloth. Animals!" she spat out at him.

Carlo flipped the cigarette away and before she could move he had pulled her again to his broad chest. "Don't you ever say that again," he snarled in a low, menancing voice. His eyes dark pools of unknown violence. Rita stared at him too frightened to speak. Her arms hung lifeless at her sides.

A small fleck of blood appeared on her swollen lower lip. Carlo's big thumb brushed it off gently. His look softening slightly. "You are some kind of girl," he repeated, more to himself than to Rita. "'Golden Girl' that's what he always called you."

Rita felt the tears she had refused to shed over Carlo's rough treatment begin to flow down her cheeks at the mention of her father again. Carlo's grip slackened at the sight of her tears.

"Well, you are what you are," he stated resignedly and releasing her, he turned and strode down the terrace steps away from the Ball.

Rita collasped on the marble bench, her sobs muffled in her pale hands. It was quite some time before she could drag herself to the Ladies Room and repair the damage Carlo had done. Her hair needed recombing and her lips several applications of cold water before the swelling disappeared and she could apply some lipstick.

"This evening is a disaster," she said to the pale, sad faced woman in blue, reflected back at her in the large mirror. She wished fervently that she had never come to Urbino. Her inheritance had brought her nothing but pain and heartache. Oh, how she yearned to be back in her quiet life in Connecticut. These mountains were beautiful but also, very treacherous. She snapped her purse shut and went out in search of David, determined to leave the Ball and the Marches immediately.

The Ball was in full swing with one orchestra blaring out a raucous rock and roll number. Rita knew she could skip looking in there for David as he abhorred any wild music. She was just about to enter the other ballroom when she almost collided with Father Vincenzo, Aunt Andrea and of all people, Carlo's parents. They all chatted amiably for a few minutes with Rita attempting to hide her uneasiness, then she excused herself to continue looking for David. She found it difficult to imagine two nicer people like the Molzas having such rotten sons. Dante and Carlo were certainly alike, even if Carlo did claim he was different. She pushed angrily through the crowd. Finally, after having little luck locating David, she returned to sit with Andrea and the Molzas. She strained, and craned her neck to catch a glimpse of David in the ever increasing crowd. 'Where could he be?,' she wondered and where were Felicianna and Dante? Were they with David? And the deSicas, she hadn't seen them since they had first arrived at the Ball.

"Damn," she cursed, "This is a rotten party," she felt lost and abandoned. Her head was starting to throb and her lip stung every time she took a sip of her Asti Spumanti.

Suddenly, she saw Inspectore Adolfo bobbing his way through the crowd, coming straight towards their table.

"Excuse me, Senore Molza, my apologies for interrupting your evening at this most festive occasion but something has come up."

He nodded somberly to Andrea and Rita. "Si, Inspectore. You must perform your duties accordingly. Please proceed," Mr. Molza stood, leaning closer to hear the Inspectore over the sounds of the dance music.

"A most tragic accident has occurred."

"Carlo!" Rita gasped standing abruptly.

"No, no, signorina. Not Carlo but Senore and Senora de Sica. Rita let out a sigh of relief and slumped down in her chair.

"They failed to negotiate the sharp curve at Mendora pass and, unfortunately, they were both killed instantly. However, Senore Molza, a most extraordinary thing," the Inspectore glanced nervously back at Rita, "The Senora deSica was found wearing this brooch under her coat on the lapel of her traveling suit," he held out the square, emerald brooch nestled in his large, white handkerchief. Rita gasped, covering her mouth with a trembling hand.

"The Signorina recognizes this particular brooch?" the Inspectore questioned Rita sternly.

"Oh, yes. I mean no. I mean…. Oh God…." Rita looked frantically at Andrea, then back to the stern faces of the Inspectore and Mario Molza.

"I think it best that we return to Villa San Giovanni, immediately." Andrea Feltre rose giving the two men a stern look of her own. "Inspectore will you please inform the others and join us later? Come, Margarita." The old woman swept Rita towards the main exit.

The ride back to the Villa was spent in shocked silence.

The cars were buffeted by a strong wind that had blown down from the mountains. Clouds were fast forming over the bright stars turning the once clear night dark and murky. Rita felt shaken to the very core of her being. She grieved for the deSicas, and rejoiced that it hadn't been Carlo dead and crushed in the wrecked car. Then a wave of guilt washed over her…my God…David! She had never even thought of him. What was happening to her? Why had she thought of Carlo and not David? Dear, sweet David. And where was he? Why wasn't he here with her? She glanced out the car window just as a great, gray cloud hid the full moon making the road a vast, dark tunnel perilously burrowing between the mountains. She shuddered, drawing her evening-wrap tight about her bare shoulders. The wind bent the tall cypress trees and whistled and hissed around the car window. Rita felt something evil flying in the angry wind. She thought it was whispering "Jewe.ls.... jewwwels.... jewwwe.ls." She couldn't stop seeing the emerald brooch as it lay green against the Inspectore's white handkerchief, And the other jewels, were they buried under the deSica's smashed car? If only she hadn't bumped into them coming back from the garden. Kay had put two and two together after spying the tortoise under her arm. 'Oh, why did I have to find those cursed jewels.' Rita sat sunk in utter desolation knowing she had, by discovering the jewels, stepped back into the past. All the terror and violence she had desperately tried to bury was back again swirling in the cold, mountain wind.

Arriving at the Villa, they found the Barlettas visibly shocked at the tragic news but managing, as usual, to keep everything under control. Sofia had coffee and brandy set out on the long, low oak table placed before the fire in the library.

Rita feeling very depressed and sensing a long night ahead, excused herself to run upstairs and change into something a bit more comfortable. Her lovely blue gown had not helped to create the wonderful, gay evening she had envisioned. Opening her bedroom door, she froze at the sight before her. The room was turned inside out, every drawer was opened, the bed ripped apart.

Her suitcases, opened and contents scattered about. It was as if some frenzied maniac had become incensed at not finding whatever he or she had been searching for. Rita scooped up her long, blue skirts and ran screaming from the ruined room.

"Inspectore, Mr. Molza, Aunt Andrea…" breathlessly she told the shocked group that had run to meet her at the bottom of the stairs.

"My room. Someone has been in my room….they…they…"

The Inspectore and Mario Molza dashed up the stairs while the women guided a trembling Rita back into the library. They all decided on a liberal glass of brandy and had just finished coaxing Rita into swallowing it when the men returned. They were joined by Ernesto, his friends, Felicianna and Dante, all shocked, all talking in low, hushed voices. The Inspectore was soon besieged by questions and finally in exasperation calling for silence.

"Thank you. Now, Signorina Margarita, I believe you have something to tell me?" his sharp little eyes bore into Rita.

She looked around her at all the expectant faces and suddenly felt very vulnerable. She wished that Carlo or David were there. But it seemed neither one was about to show up.

Aunt Andrea gave her an encouraging nod and Rita began her story of finding the hidden compartment in the tortoise. Inspectore Adolfo nodded affirmatively several times, stroked his double chin; then bounced to his feet, startling everyone.

"The American. This David Swan, he was at the Ball tonight?" he questioned Rita.

"Why, yes. Of course David was there. Why do you ask?" she felt a small alarm go off inside her stomach.

"Because, Signorina Bondone, if the deSicas did find the jewels and intended to flee to America, where ARE the jewels?

They were not found in the wreckage! Only this large emerald, that Senora deSica had pinned to her lapel and then covered over by her coat on this cool evening. So, I ask, again...where are the jewels?"

Rita looked helplessly at the Inspectore. Her mouth moved but no sounds came forth. She sat confused and very frightened. A tight ball of fear growing larger in her stomach.

"Surely, Inspectore, you don't believe Margarita has anything at all to do with this." Andrea now stood with her frail hand protectively on Rita's trembling shoulder.

Inspectore Adolfo rolled back on his small feet. "But of course not. Please. My apologies for upsetting her," he clasped Rita's cold hands, "Unfortunately, the Poliza suspects a third party may be involved, may even have helped the deSicas to their untimely deaths."

There were gasps and murmurs around the quiet room. The Inspectore dropped Rita's hands, spreading his own pudgy ones.

"So, we must locate this David Swan," he concluded.

Rita looked around the library at all the faces watching her. They seemed strangers once more. Now, they were accusing

David and maybe even her, of murder! Yes, she could see it in their eyes. They were condemning her, Rita Bond. They were going to punish her, not just for this but for that other moon-lit night long ago. When she had run away, run away from Villa Sera, run away from being Margarita Bondone.

She leaped to her feet. Her head throbbed painfully, her right vision was blurring, making the room seem strangely unbalanced. She whirled, lashing out at them all. "David would never do such a thing. Never! Do you hear me?" she screamed. She felt so hot and feverish, swaying and almost falling.

Senore Molza stepped forward to help her. "And you..." she turned on him "You, what about your son. What about Carlo? Where is he?" she swept the room with a shaking arm flung out. "Carlo and his henchmen. They probably took the damn jewels"

Andrea Feltre burst into tears and covered her face with her thin, bony hands. Rita felt tears spring to her own hazy eyes but she couldn't stop herself. She wanted to lash out and hurt them all for dragging her back into this turbulent life.

"Yes, Carlo. He is very good driving on those sharp curves.... he," a figure in ruby velvet rushed forward pinning Rita's crazy flapping arms to her side and whispering calmly in her ear "Mio dios, Rita you don't know what you are saying!"

Felicianna's soft soothing voice was the last thing Rita heard as she slumped into her new friend's arms.

Chapter 14

For the next few days, Rita drifted in and out of conciousness. Her uneasy sleep troubled by the recurring dream of two men struggling in the moonlit garden. Gentle hands always stopped the frightened, futile thrashing as Felicianna maintained her vigil. Dr. Cuneo made several visits. Rita was barely concious of his firm, professional touch. His tiny light probed the darkness of her closed eyes. Until one sunny morning, she awoke to stare back into his concerned eyes. Greatly relieved to have his patient fully alert again, Doctor Cuneo left detailed instructions with his nurse who had shared the bedside vigil with Felicianna.

Gradually, Rita regained her strength except for her right vision, which was very weak and would remain so for several months necessitating the use of eye-glasses. Her fall after the shooting had done more damage to her right eye than the Doctor had first diagnosed. He had called an eye specialist, a Doctor

Tano, who prescribed drops and the new glasses. With time, in a few months her vision would be back to normal, he assured her. She sat up in bed, now, with the new glasses framing her crystal blue eyes, her sketch-pad propped on her knees. As she put the finishing touches on a charcoal sketch of Villa Sera, Rita was vastly relieved to know she could still work with her impaired vision. She also was immensely relieved to know that the Villa was finally sold. Dominic Mattini had completed all the legal paperwork and Rita had made a handsome profit on the sale. The Ambassador Realty Company now owned Villa Sera and she was finally free. She sighed deeply, gazing at her sketch pad. She had captured the isolation of the small Villa nestled down on the mountainside. It's strange beauty intrigued and repelled her at the same time. She laid aside her large sketch pad. She wanted nothing more but to return to her cozy Connecticut apartment, back to her safe, quiet job at the Museum.

She stared out the window, the sunlight sifted amongst the stunted olive trees creating a nebulous scene far down the mountainside. She shivered.

'Yes,' she thought bitterly, 'that is The Marches, shadowy and obscure just like her terrible nightmares even in broad daylight.'

Damn, where was David? She missed him and needed his cool, clear thinking. She didn't for one minute believe he had anything to do with the deSica, or the missing jewels. Yet, it was so unlike him to go off like this and he had seemed rather strange at the Ball. She knew the Polizia were searching for him but she still believed it was all a mistake. David had only just met the deSicas and he had never shown any inclination towards material possessions. Was, in fact, very moderate in his purchases. Even reprimanding her on several occasions for her own extravagant purchases. No, David must have a logical reason for leaving so abruptly. Probably, something to do with his insurance job. He was far too conscientious about his work. Rita lay wearily back on the pillows, her temples throbbing with the effort of trying to sort out all the pieces of the shooting, cousin Paul's arrest, discovering the jewels only to have them disappear again and the deSicas accident or murder, as the Inspectore hinted. It saddened her to think that it was far more logical that Carlo was somehow involved with the deSicas and the theft of the jewels from the Fountain of the Tortoises. After all, hadn't he followed her there? Maybe he had bumped against the tortoise during his fight with Dante, loosening it enough so that his curiosity was aroused, then returning later to find the hidden jewels. Rita sighed and turned restlessly on the bed. She remembered how Felicianna and Father Vincenzo had been aghast at her accusations against Carlo. They were all so very loyal towards Carlo. She felt a warm flush as she remembered his soft, gentle kisses. His warm flashing, dark eyes. If only he would stay that way for more than five minutes. Hot tears eased from her aching eyes. No, it was impossible!

Carlo was brash, headstrong and violent. She had only to think of the beating he had given Dante. To remember the brutal kiss the night of the Museum Ball. Yes, Carlo was certainly the type capable of theft and murder. Everyone knew he was an expert driver and the winding, treacherous mountain roads were no hardship for him. And the Inspectore could not locate Carlo at any of his usual haunts, so where was he? If he was so innocent as Felicianna, Father Vincenzo and Aunt Andrea proclaimed—why didn't he come forward? It was all so confusing. Why had she finally met two handsome, successful men only to have them BOTH drop out of her life so mysteriously? Rita finally drifted off into a dream filled sleep in which both Carlo and David now wrestled the hooded figures of her childhood nightmares. David's cool lips would press her own fevered ones only to be suddenly replaced by Carlo's hot, persistent lips and probing tongue. Rita moaned and thrashed in her tangled blankets, and the sun drenched afternoon turned slowly into a dark, starless night.

Several days later, the quiet, somber group sitting around the long, candlelit dining table was a far cry from the laughing, boisterous group Rita had encountered on her first night in Urbino. Aunt Andrea looked distressingly pale and sat slumped at the head of the long table. Frail and all but lost in the large oak chair. She toyed with the food on her plate.

"We will miss you, Margarita," her voice barely a whisper.

"Oh, Andrea I'll miss you, too," Rita patted the black gowned arm. Surprised and shocked at how terribly thin her aunt had gotten in the short time she had been there.

"Can't I convince you to remain here at Villa San Giovanni?"

"No, Aunt Andrea. I MUST get on with my own life. I have to return to Connecticut before I lose my job," Rita answered firmly. She was determined to pick up the pieces of her small life. With the money from the sale of the Villa Sera she could now enroll in the Art classes at the University. She really did not need her job now, but she was reluctant to give it up just yet. It was her sanctuary from the madness of the Bondone curse. There she was plain, American Rita Bond. No, she had to return and quickly, if she was to maintain her sanity.

"But you must return next Spring for our wedding," Felicianna pleaded, as she sat breathtakingly beautiful in a black gown with a soft ruffled collar blending into the dark, thick curls cascading around her lovely, worried face.

"Of course, Felicianna. I wouldn't miss your wedding!" Rita smiled fondly back as some of the worry vanished from the other girl's face to be replaced by a flicker of a smile.

"Oh, Margarita, I wish I could tell…" but before Felicianna could continue she was rudely interrupted by Dante who sat gloomily beside her.

"Basta, enough! You know his wishes. You will obey, and silence your foolish tongue, you silly woman!"

Felicianna's dark eyes flashed angrily back at her husband-to-be. Rita thought happily that she was about to defy him but much to her surprise, Felicianna glanced quickly at Andrea then turned angrily back to her dinner. Stabbing a good-size piece of beef she filled her mouth, preventing any further words from escaping.

"Well, I shall be only to happy to drive you down to the airport in the morning, Rita," Ernesto's soothing voice broke the awkward silence.

"Why, thank you, Ernesto. I'm very grateful." Rita was relieved it would be the pleasant, open, uncomplicated Ernesto that would accompany her on the long drive. She really enjoyed his company. He had surprised her with a vast knowledge of the art world. His family background gave him access to the intrigues of all the top museums secret financial deals, and his unorthodox personal life allowed him to rub elbows with many of Europe's up and coming artists. His stories fascinated Rita and she was pleased the long ride would be made pleasant by Ernesto's presence. She remembered only too well her terrifying ride up the mountain on her arrival. How very uncomfortable she had been.... forced to sit so close in the small sports car, touching the big, sullen, rock-faced Carlo. How frightened she was when the black Alfetta tried to force them off the high mountain road. Rita shivered. She squeezed her eyes shut as if to block out the ugly scene.

"Margarita, are you all right?" a soft, warm hand covered Rita's shaking one, as Andrea leaned forward, worry lining her sad face.

"Yes, Andrea, I'm fine. Would you excuse me now? I must finish packing." Rita bade the others a hasty good-night and retreated, shivering to her cool room. She undressed and crawled miserably into the cold bed. Her thoughts raced madly around in her tired head. What had Felicianna wanted to tell her? Why had the others silenced her? Could it have been about Carlo? She felt sure they were all protecting him. Naturally, he was one of their own. She thought of his big, strong hands straining on the steering wheel. The same wide hands smashing into Dante's stunned face, lifting her and crushing her tight against his big chest as he carried her back to her room. Oh, no. No, I don't want to think about any of that! It's all over. When I get back to the States I'm sure David will contact me. She sensed somehow that David's disappearance was connected to Carlo in some puzzling way. Her thoughts whirled back to the many happy, calm evenings she had spent with David. The intimate dinners in the cozy little "Captain's Wheel" restaurant overlooking the Mystic River. How kind and gentle David had been. How patient with her. It was really because of David that she had finally forsaken her recluse life and begun to live as other young, attractive women her age.

She was shivering uncontrollably now. Just thinking back to her parent's accident, then her fiancee's tragic death and now the deSica's awful murder thoroughly convinced her that the Bondone curse was going to haunt her all her life. There was no escape!

A soft knock on the door startled her. It was one of the maids, apologizing profusely because she hadn't prepared the Signorina's bed early enough. She slipped a cloth-covered hot water bottle under the bedcovers at Rita's feet. Meekly handing the second one to Rita, she again apologized, making a hasty exit.

As the door closed on the cool, damp room, Rita clutched the warm bottle to her chilly chest. The heat immediately radiated around her numb hands and arms, through her breasts and down to her icy hips. One more day and she would be back home. Back to her quiet routine job. Her warm, central-heated apartment. Thank God. And David. Sweet David. He would call with a rational explanation for his abrupt departure and she could forget Italy, Urbino, Villa Sera and the Bondone curse. Yes, she thought warmly, pulling the lower hot-water bottle up from her feet towards her still chilly knees and thighs. Maybe, she could thwart the ugly curse if she and David lived quietly in Connecticut. With this hopeful thought in mind, she fell into a warm, dreamy sleep. Visions of a small white house in the suburbs with two small children clutching her skirts. Normal, wonderful suburban life. Waving good-bye to David as he ran to catch the morning train. Rita relaxed, moving contentedly in her now warm bed. Her knees relaxed their hold on the warm rubber bottle and it slipped up between her thighs. Immediately, the suburban scene shattered, to be replaced by the rugged face of Carlo Molza. As the heat spread throughout Rita's lower body, images of Carlo's big body intruded into her sleepy mind. His hot lips pressed violently down on her soft, helpless lips, his dark eyes bore into her at first, softly pleading and then fiercely demanding. Rita tossed in her feverish sleep, inadvertently allowing the other hot-water bottle to slide from her already burning breasts down to her now throbbing stomach. As she lay encased by the heat above and below her sensitive area, Rita's body betrayed her and drew her into swirling, tormented dreams dominated by the dark, forceful Carlo Molza.

Chapter 15

The next morning, Rita remained unusually silent on the ride to the airport. She let Ernesto babble on, giving her puzzled looks every so often. She couldn't shake the strange feelings she had awoken with early this morning. She vaguely remembered her troubled dreams. She had been happy, contented with David and, then, Carlo had intervened. It was very confusing. She blushed, remembering her body's aching response to Carlo's hot caresses. She glanced quickly at Ernesto, praying he would not notice her shame. She felt her cheeks flaming but was happy to see that Ernesto kept his eyes on the winding road. At the airport, she bid farewell to him promising to return for Felicianna's wedding. As the silver 747 roared into the white clouds, Rita looked down at her last look at Italy. Tears filled her eyes as she thought of Felicianna. How beautiful she will look in her wedding dress. Rita felt so guilty, making hollow promises was not her style, but she knew deep inside herself that she could never return to "The Marches." Just this brief visit to sell the Villa had brought more death, more heartache. No, she could never return—the memories were too painful.

Not surprisingly, Rita's re-entry into the placid routine of Museum research did not quell her strange uneasiness. She snapped at her co-workers, she made several careless mistakes in cataloging ancient Etruscian pottery and she couldn't seem to eat and found herself having several glasses of wine before retiring, that way she slept through the night without anymore tortured dreams.

Finally, she received a short note from David, explaining how he had been called home on business, as she had angrily tried to tell Inspectore Adolio. A multi-million dollar fraud case involving several large insurance companies had blown wide open and David's expertise had been needed. She was eagerly looking forward to seeing him this evening. She missed his tall, lanky frame, his boyish grin. How handsome he had looked the last time she had seen him at the Musuem Ball. She frowned as she recalled the last sharp look he had given her. So unlike David.... but he must have known then that he had to return. The fraud case must have been on his mind even then. How so like him not to upset her with the news that he had to return to the States. She smiled fondly, planning a nice candlelight dinner for him that evening.

The first snow of the season had quietly covered the

Musuem's employee parking lot. As Rita prepared to unlock her Datsun, her eyes fell to the many footprints around her own wet feet. Someone had been standing right here. Trying to open her car? She wondered. She inspected the lock and decided it had not been tampered with. But, she still glanced nervously into the back seat. It was empty. Both doors were still securely locked. Puzzled, she finished unlocking the door and slipped into the cold car. She turned the key in the ignition, flipped on the windshield wipers and caught a glimpse of several figures, head down against the bitter wind, hurrying out to their snow-covered cars. 'Probably someone dashed up to the wrong car in their haste to get out of the storm,' she thought as she backed out and drove slowly onto Federal Street. She headed North then took a sharp left onto Chilton Avenue where she skidded dangerously close to an oncoming car. Rita clenched the steering wheel tighter. The windshield wipers were barely clearing a small spot for her to see out. The snow swirled in crazy patterns completely blinding one minute, then blowing away the next. She tugged at the defroster knob, snapped up the heater fan and cursed herself for not having the snow tires put on last week. Turning left again she crawled along Mystic Avenue where the traffic was thinning out. Most of the folks who lived in the Greenvale suburb drove out by way of Route 124, but Rita loved the longer, winding Mystic Avenue, which ran alongside the wide, choppy Mystic River. Usually, the lights flickering on the water was a calming sight to Rita's tense nerves after a day of dusty research in the bowels of the Musuem.

But tonight, the few lights were barely visible in the white whirling mass.

"You, Fool!" she spoke aloud in the small Datsun. "You should have taken the Expressway tonight. This is going to take hours."

She concentrated on trying to keep the constantly disappearing road in sight. High beams from behind flashed in her rear view mirror. The constant brightness distracted her, bothered her eyes.

"Dim them, you idiot," she cursed out loud. But the lights continued to bore down on her. She drove slowly and cautiously, feeling her light car skid several times; she braked slightly while the second time her foot went all the way to the floor.

"Oh, my God!" She pumped the brake but it was useless. She was just at the approach ramp to the Gillettee Bridge when a large shape loomed to her right; a car was pulling right in front of her. Rita had no choice but to pull the steering wheel sharply to the left. She felt her Datsun leave the road and saw below her the dark, icy water as her head-lights pierced the white thickness. She felt a horror and terror even worse than what she had felt on the mountain road in Italy when the other small car had hung so precariously on the precipice of death. Then she had Carlo. Now, she was terrifyingly alone. As the car hurtled toward certain icy death, a wheel hit a boulder half buried under the drifting snow, slowing down the hurtling car. Rita screamed as she was thrown about inside the dark car. She prayed, calling out to her dead parents.

"No, please, Mama. Not this! Papa not drowning! No...no...no. Please God, help me," she pleaded and prayed. Her absolute terror of drowning, for she had relived her parents drowning a thousand times over as a young girl, propelled her to action and she pushed frantically on the car door, forcing it open and flinging herself out into the cold, snow-covered embankment. Rolling and tumbling in the cold snow, her last thoughts were of Carlo Molza.... how wonderfully warm she had been when he had held her close!

"Hey, lady. Hey, wake up. You OK?"

Rita smelled leather and opened her eyes to stare into the concerned eyes of a burly truck driver. His hair and jacket wet with snow.

"Lady, I was right behind you. I saw that bastard cut you off. But, you just shot over the side like a bat out of hell. What happened?" he tried to shield her face from the fast, falling snow.

"No brakes. No brakes," she mumbled numbly.

"Well, no wonder. You are a lucky lady, miss, 'cause you won't be driving that little shit-box again." Rita followed his gaze to the river where a few bubbles betrayed the final resting place of her little Datsun. She groaned.

"Hey, any broken bones, lady?" worry creased his beefy face.

"Oh, no, nothing broken. Just more bruises. Please, can you help me up."

"Lady, I called the cops on the CB when I saw you going over. They'll be here with an Ambulance any minute."

"Please, look I'm fine," she struggled to her feet. "We'll freeze down here. I'm so cold." She began to shake uncontrollably, her teeth chattering. She began to try to climb back up the high embankment.

"OK, Lady, if you say so." A beefy hand grabbed her arm and half-carried her up through the deep snow. By the time they reached the top, Rita's nylon clad legs were stiff and useless. She was in a semiconscious state, barely aware of the flashing lights of the ambulance, she felt herself being bundled into something warm and then she slipped into black darkness.

She awoke hours later to find David sitting by her side.

"You poor darling," he whispered, brushing her lips with his own cool lips. "We should have arranged to meet in town. You never should have tried to drive on such a rotten night."

Rita stared numbly at David. His words left her strangely unmoved. She looked deeply into his vacant blue eyes. His even voice droned on with endearments but his eyes remained cool and detached. A chilly tremor ran through her as his long, slender fingers traced a deep scratch on her right cheek.

She heard not a word he was saying, so chilled and numb did she feel at his touch. They were interrupted by a smiling, young nurse briskly entering the stark hospital room. She beamed at the blond, handsome David, handed Rita a tiny paper-cup with two pills and then poured some water from the bedside carafe into a larger paper-cup.

"All the way down, Miss Bond. You will feel much better in

the morning. You have had a bad scare but you'll be fine after a few days rest."

Rita obediently swallowed the pills as the pretty, young nurse watched her. Rita could see David out of the corner of her eye, he was watching the nurse. His blue eyes were sparkling and animated. She realized, suddenly, that he never looked at her that way. Heavy-hearted, she handed the nurse the empty cup; she, in turn, smiled happily, picked up her tray of tiny pill cups and breezed out of the room. Rita was relieved that she did not shut the door completely. Somehow, it made her feel safer with the door opened. She brought her sleepy gaze back to David's face. Again, he was saying something about when she got out of the hospital but she simply could not concentrate on his words. She watched his handsome face. Strange, how utterly void of expression it was. The boyish grin she had loved so just a few weeks ago now seemed almost ludicrous. His long hands clasped Rita's and she had to fight a tremendous urge to pull her hands away. She noticed a greasy smudge on his right thumb and his nails were dirty. She stared at the grease and the tiny black flecks under his, usually immaculate, nails and she became filled with dread.

'Yes,' she thought, 'I'm afraid of him. I must stay awake.' She fought against the increasingly sleepy haze that threatened to draw her under. She raised her eyes to David's face and it was a stranger looking back at her. She tried to speak but her voice came out a pitiful squeak. She pulled her hands free and attempted to push herself up in the bed.

"No, no, my child. Don't try to sit up," Father Vincenzo strode purposely across the hospital room. He kissed her gently on the forehead, and Rita smelt his warm Amaretto scented breath and relaxed back on her pillow.

"Wha...aa... What are you doing here?" she thought she sounded drunk.

"Well, I am here for the Conference of International Religions." Father Vincenzo turned giving David a long strange look.

"Well, darling, I must be going. I'll come by for you in the morning." David gave her another cool kiss on the cheek and left the room quickly. Rita watched his tall frame disappear and uttering a sigh of relief turned her tear-filled eyes back to Father Vincenzo. His kind, lined face leaned close.

"There, there, my dear. You are safe now. We never should have allowed you to leave Urbino." He patted her arm and then pulled a chair close to the bed. Mutterring under his breath, he settled down with his worn, black prayer book.

"I shall be here all night, my dear, so don't you be the least bit frightened. We should have listened to Carlo," he shook his old head sadly and began his soft litany of prayers.

The old priest's presence beside her and the mention of Carlo, released Rita from her rigid, unknown fears and she slowly drifted off into a deep sleep.

Hushed voices arguing right outside her door, woke Rita the next morning. She saw Father Vincenzo and a smocked-clad doctor standing there. She could tell by the Doctor's uncertain expression that Father Vincenzo was excerting his considerable charm and vast persuasive powers to convince the Doctor that whatever he, Father Vincenzo, wanted was the correct procedure to follow. Finally, the weary Doctor nodded his consent and hurried away.

"Ah, my dear, you are feeling better, I pray?" Father Vincenzo turned back into the room, smiling broadly at Rita.

"Oh, yes, Father. What was that all about?" she nodded weakly towards the open door.

"The good Doctor has consented to discharge you into my care. So as soon as you have some nourishment we will have the nurse help you dress and be away from this institution," he waved his veined hand at the sterile, stark hospital room. Rita glanced around her, seeing the room for the first time. The beige walls and floors were rather drab compared to the gorgeous tapestries and paintings at Villa San Giovanni.

"Yes, I do want to leave and right away," she could not tell him that it wasn't just the depressing hospital room but, also, her fear that David would return, that caused her to want to be as far away as possible.

"Here, now, this will do wonders for you, my dear," he indicated the overloaded breakfast tray that the nurse was placing on the table. The delicious aroma of hot coffee filled the room and Rita realized she was ravenous. The pretty nurse had even brought enough eggs, sausages and muffins for Father Vincenzo.

She smiled her lovely, warm smile and hurried off. Rita attacked the food, each mouthful brought renewed strength to her bruised body. As soon as she had swallowed the last mouthful, she threw back the covers, slid her legs over the edge of the bed and slid to the floor. The sight of her swollen, black and blue legs shocked her and she held to the bed for support as dizzyness swept over her. Father Vincenzo stood quickly, dropping his egg-laden fork. "No, no, my dear. Wait for the nurse," he pressed the buzzer for the nurse.

Too late, Rita realized her bare backside was exposed to the embarrassed priest. She had been so shocked to see her legs swollen almost twice their normal size she had allowed the hospital johnny to gape open in the back. They were both relieved when the nurse arrived and helped her into the bathroom where she attempted to dress.

It was sometime later, when she emerged looking not much better but at least dressed for the street. Her clothes were torn and she did not have any stockings on but she had managed to get her swollen feet into white cotton hospital socks and paper slippers. Her hair was brushed back from her injured face which was as white as the ground outside the hospital and she was happy to see that the snow had finally stopped, as she was wheeled out and whisked into a waiting limousine. At the airport they boarded a sleek, private jet. Rita was far too weak to even care where she was going or even, who, owned the luxurious plane that roared into the morning sun, carrying her away from the cold, snow-covered streets of Connecticut. She slept almost continuously, gaining consciousness just long enough to swallow fluids handed to her by a gray-haired nurse. Rita knew she was badly bruised and battered physically for she ached all over. But, it was her mind she was concerned about. Awake the terror returned. The sharp crack of the gunshot, the sight of David moving away from her falling body and, now, the grease and dirt on his hands, all these things haunted her. She fought against the idea that David had tampered with the brakes on her Datsun but the thought kept getting stronger. Remembering the warm look he had given the pretty, young nurse and comparing that to the vacant, emotionless manner he had with her, she realized, all her female instincts were trying to tell her something. David was decidedly cool and detached. But, subconsciously, she must have wanted him that way. She had been safe from any real relationship with David. He never really touched her emotions. Her passions could lie dormant with David. Not so with Carlo Molza. Carlo's quick mood changes left her confused and emotionally drained. The unleashed fury, the raw disgust blazing from his dark eyes as he roughly dropped her on the bed after the near rape by Dante. All these violent reactions frightened her. She could not understand why everything she did came out wrong where Carlo was concerned. She clearly remembered, now, the tall young teenager who had grabbed the terrified child, with the long, blond hair streaming in the night wind, and raced up the dark, mountain path. He had tried to hold her, to shelter her, but the others had come and tore her away from his warm arms.

"Never tell. Never, never tell!" her beautiful mother entreated with tears streaming down her lovely, pale face. "Your Papa. Your Papa. Oh, my God! Mio Dios," she had pressed the young child to her sobbing, heaving breast. And, to this day, the fragrance of "Lucianna" perfume evoked fearful feelings of suffocation in Rita. She knew, now, that when she finally saw her father much later that evening, she had been so relived to see him alive that her young mind had obeyed her tearful mother and completely blocked out the entire episode of the struggle in the moonlit garden. What did it matter, who the fallen man was, as long as it was not her Papa. Now, in her strange, confused state of mind after all these years, she suddenly wondered who WAS the stranger who fought so savagely against her father? Who was the dead man laying at the bloodied feet of the young girl, herself, in her tortured dreams? Somehow, she must find out. It seemed important that she know his identity. That knowledge, that man's identity was like a thin thread weaving through her fevered, frightened half-crazed brain.

Each time she dozed off the thought was stronger. The thin thread became a rope which she tried repeatedly to grasp only to be thwarted by images of David and Carlo, struggling for possession of the illusive swaying rope.

The next few days were lost to Rita's exhausted mind. So safe and secure did she feel with Father Vincenzo and the other tall, dark man who occassionally leaned over her that she just let herself drift off, time and time again. She struggled to gain complete consciousness, especially when the other man, with the deep soothing voice, stood over her. Finally, on the third day, the deep voice drew her to the brink of consciousness and she opened her eyes. Carlo bent close to her. A gentle smile on his big, rugged face. He kissed her lips softly.

"Hello, darling. Welcome back."

Rita gave him a weak smile. The dark eyes beaming down at her told her in a thousand ways she belonged to him. There would be no escaping, this time.

"Wh…where have you been?" she whispered, somewhat angrily.

"Later, sweetheart. I will fill you in on everything. I'm sorry I had to leave without a proper Good-bye but events took a much quicker turn than we had figured on. But, rest assured, I am never letting you out of my sight from now on," he brushed back a strand of hair from her bruised face. His fingers were strong and warm and sent pleasurable sensations through her sore body. She had no desire to shrink from his touch, as she had David's. Rather, she pressed her cheek into the palm of his big hand.

"Carlo, Carlo," she felt tears spring to her eyes.

"No, No, darling. Please don't cry," he gathered her in his strong arms. He rocked her gently, while his voice, broken and filled with anguish, he whispered, "God, why did I ever leave you? I almost lost you! What a stupid fool I have been." He was kissing her hair, then her forehead, her eyes, her tear-stained cheeks and finally her lips. A kiss so soft, so gentle yet so firm and insistent, it left no doubt in Rita's mind that with Carlo she would be forced to use all her emotions, all her buried passions. She smiled up at him.

"I am crying because I'm so happy you are here. So happy you are back. Don't ever leave me again, please," she kissed him again, firmly and possessively and she saw a gleam come into his dark eyes. She drew away.

"Now, out with you. I know I must be a mess. I need a comb, some lipstick, some…"

"Whoa, young lady," Carlo grinned happily. "I see you are feeling better, more like your old self. But, first, we will have the Doctor in here then we'll see about make-up and such. Besides, you are beautiful without all that stuff." He kissed her soundly and yelling happily at the top of his powerful lungs, bounded out of the room. In rapid succession, Rita saw the Doctor, Father Vincenzo, and, to her amazement and joy, both Aunt Andrea and Aunt Louisa-Maria. The two old ladies fluttered around Rita. Brushing her tangled hair, lending her their sweet, lavender cologne and a soft, pink lipstick. Aunt Andrea even brought her a beautiful lilac-colored bed jacket. Slipping it over Rita's shoulders, she arranged the wide lace collar around Rita's thin, pale face.

"Margarita, dear, we must fatten you up, some. You are so thin," she gave Rita a dry kiss on the cheek.

"Don't be silly, Andrea. That is the fashion now-a-days. All the young girls are pencil-thin," retorted Louisa-Maria.

"Well, men like curves!" snapped back Andrea.

"Humph. What do you know about men? Things are a lot different now, then when we were young," the two old ladies glared at each other and were interrupted by the arrival of Carlo carrying a huge tray loaded with sandwiches, coffee and a decanter of Amaretto di Saronno. Carlo winked at Rita as he set the tray down and began pouring the coffee, laced with generous shots of Amaretto. Rita could tell by the warm glow in his dark eyes that he was pleased with her meager attempt to freshen up. The sandwiches soon disappeared, washed down with several Amaretto coffees and before long everyone was chattering at once.

"Enough. Enough!" Father Vincenzo put his cup down, and raised both hands for silence. "With your permission Carlo....?" he nodded toward Carlo, waiting for his consent.

After what seemed a very long moment Carlo rose, walked over to Rita's bed, clasped her hand tightly in his own and in a strong, clear voice chocked with emotion proclaimed.

"I love you, Margarita. I guess I have for years." he turned, walked over to the long window and with his back to the room instructed firmly, "Proceed, Father Vincenzo."

"Gracie, Carlo," the old priest began pacing at the foot of the big bed. He began his story way back on that fateful night when Rita was an unfortunate witness to her father's life threatening struggle. She finally learned the deadman's identity. He was Mario Cigno.

Father Vincenzo continued, "Although, everyone in the family knew the jewels were hidden somewhere on Villa Sera, all agreed it was better to leave them hidden forever. When your parents flew to the States, hoping to leave behind the terrible memories, they had no idea the evil would find them there. They had been very concerned about their young daughter, for you had stopped speaking during the day and you screamed out in your sleep every night," he looked sadly at Rita. "Unfortunately, the terrible Bondone curse followed your family."

"No!" Carlo whirled around to glare at Father Vincenzo. "A priest should not speak of curses!" he strode over to sit on the edge of Rita's bed. His muscular arms dangled between his knees. He gave her a helpless, aching look. Rita reached for his arm, wanting to comfort him; yet knowing it should be the other way around. She waited tensely for the shaking, old priest to continue. The two Aunts sat quietly sipping their coffee. Although, she was eager to hear the whole story, she was once again frightened to the very core of her being. An air of anxious finality hung heavy in the still room. When the old priest continued to stand silently, his hands clasped as if in prayer, Rita turned to Carlo, "Please, Carlo. I must know. I'm a grown woman, now. I can face whatever it is. When you found me on the path, I was just a child.... a hysterical child, to be sure. But, now, that child is a woman and I have a right to know.... if only to protect myself."

"I will protect you," Carlo declared, his dark eyes flashed and his big hands clenched into hard fists.

"We know, my son," intervened Father Vincenzo. "You can protect her from further physical harm but what about the dark fears and terrors inside her?"

The two old ladies nodded and pursed their thin lips. The tired priest drew himself up and continued, "Only when evil is faced can evil be conquered. Too many of us have suffered with this thing. This cancer that spreads from generation to generation. No, I tell you, Carlo, it must be stopped now! By the truth! Margarita is young but she has proven how strong she is by the very near tragedies she has survived. She has earned the right to know, Carlo." Father Vincenzo glared back at the younger man. The two men, one old and wise, one young and strong, fought a silent battle of wills. No one moved. They barely breathed. Rita felt as if time was standing still. She sensed her very future hung in the balance between these two glaring men. Slowly, Carlo, finally nodded his head.

"Grazie, my son. You do the right thing. God be with you always." The old priest made a quick sign of the cross. Then resumed his pacing back and forth. It was as if the pacing made it easier to speak of the long, hidden past.

"So, Margarita, the terrible death of your parents, the tragic accident of your fiancee, they were not so," Father Vincenzo blurted it out. He seemed immensely relieved until he stared at Rita's blank face. "Don't you understand child? They were not accidents…." he hesitated uncertain whether to continue. Then drawing a deep breath he said firmly, "It was murder!"

"Murder. Murder?" Rita whispered in a shocked voice, she looked helplessly at Carlo.

"By the same evil family bent on eternal revenge.... the Cignos," Father Vincenzo shook his fist in the air. The two Aunts were crying softly into their lace hankies. Rita noticed clearly the filigree pattern on the lace. The enormity of this piece of information was slowly seeping into her consciousness. "My parents.... the sailboat. How? How could it be murder? They drowned during a storm."

Carlo reached for her cold hand, held it tightly. "Margarita, the boat had been tampered with. My father suspected foul play the minute he heard of the accident and we flew immediately to the Cape. When the Coast Guard towed the boat in, battered though it was, we found certain evidence that the compass and radio had been cleverly altered. Your father was an expert sailing man and he would have put into shore immediately if he had known a storm as severe as that one was heading his way. Our marine experts discovered all this clever tampering with the compass and radio but the police were never able to come up with any leads to who was responsible."

Tears flowed from Rita's anguished blue eyes. Mourning her beloved parents, she clearly remembered the tanned and handsome young couple kissing her good-by with the taste of the salty ocean on their laughing lips. She had remained on the sandy beach to share a clam-bake with some young friends.... but later the wind changed, black clouds rolled in and a heavy rain sent everyone scurrying off the sandy beach. The sudden summer storm thrashed the Cape for the rest of the evening. Rita shuddered at the thought of the dark, angry waters finally dragging her parents down to a cold, watery grave. "So, it was that dead man's family? Is that what you mean? They're responsible? But it was an accident.... that man hit his head when he fell. I saw it! I saw it!" Rita's voice rose hysterically.

'They are, also, suspected in your fiancee's death," Father Vincenzo added. He seemed to want it all said and said quickly. "Why, we are not sure. It's the first time an innocent outsider has been hurt by the Bondone curse."

"Damn it!" cursed Carlo, leaping to his feet. "Enough talk of this blasted curse! The man is insane, that's all. He's the last living Cigno and he wants to be sure the Bondone family dies out before the Cigno family."

"The man...you mean it's only one man doing all these terrible things?" Rita asked incredously. She had imagined a vast stealthy army of black clad men.

"Well, he did induce your cousin, Paul, to join him. Paul had gotten involved with the Red Brigands. They wanted the jewels to help finance their terrorist activities. And, I suppose, he knew the Red Brigands would kill Paul once they had the jewels." Father Vincenzo poured himself another coffee. "Ladies?" he gestured to the two Aunts, who sat stiff as stone statues. Aunt Andrea blinked, nodded yes.

"Just some Arnaretto, please," requested Aunt Louisa-Maria, "Poor Paul. I always knew he'd come to no damn good!"

"Louisa-Maria," whispered a shocked Andrea, daintily pressing her dry, cracked lips with the lace hanky.

"This Cigno…this last man, this insane monster who is he?" Rita looked pleadingly at Carlo. Dreading his answer for she had suddenly remembered her Italian.

"David Swan," Carlo answered bitterly.

"Of course. Cigno means swan in Italian. I've been so stupid. So blind!" she sat rigidly in the bed. No tears flowed now from her burning, feverish eyes. Carlo went to her and clasped her in his strong, muscular arms. His worried eyes searched her taunt face.

"You had no way of knowing. Don't blame yourself for anything, Margarita," he hugged her to his big chest. Rita longed to remain close in his arms forever. She didn't want to move, or speak or think. Especially think. She despised herself for ever being with David Swan. She hated herself for kissing those treacherous, lying lips, for ever allowing those murderous hands to even touch her.

"Oh, God, Carlo," she threw her arms around him. Thrusting herself closer to his warm body. "Hold me. Hold me! Please," she begged him.

"Shh, shh, Darling. I'll hold you. I'll always hold you. I've wanted to hold you for years. They made me—stay away. They were all afraid the sight of me would trigger your memory. Everyone was so afraid for your sanity. Oh, darling, I knew I should have followed my instincts." He was kissing her forehead. "I've loved you all these years from afar. Every time I came to the East coast I made sure I saw you from a distance. It was hell, Margarita. Pure hell. But now I have you. I'll never let you go!" he pressed his hot lips gently on Rita's trembling lips.

"Ahem," a discreet cough reminded Carlo of the others present in the now darkening room. He stood.

"You must rest now, Rita. This has all been a terrible shock but you had to know for your own safety," he pulled the covers up and tucked them gently under her chin.

"Yes, Margarita. You see we can not prove anything against Swan. He is extremely clever and very careful. But now he realizes that-we know who he is, so he may get careless." Father Vincenzo explained quietly. "You will be much safer here at Carlo's where we have men to guard the grounds." He smiled kindly at the stunned girl.

"Yes, darling, and we will be here also," the two old ladies glided up to the bed. Each kissed Rita and she could see tears glistening in their tired eyes. So many, many years, Rita thought. They've lived through all this evil curse. Oh, God, please let it end. Somehow. And soon. Soon.

The doctor entered the room after everyone had filed solemnly out. He insisted on giving Rita another shot but she begged him, "No, please. I've had enough drugs in the hospital, I'll be fine. I just need to rest a bit."

He indulged her but left some tablets on the bedside table with instructions for Rita to take two if she became too distraught to sleep.

Strangely enough she did fall asleep. When she awoke, it was after midnight. She lay thinking. Her thoughts were as dark as the night. Her hatred for David was a cold, icy core hardening inside her breast. The murdering beast! How could she have been taken in by him? She had been timid. That was it... she rationalized. She hadn't wanted a real relationship. She had been afraid after Bob was killed. She didn't want to be hurt again. That's why she had been taken in by David. Cool, undemanding David. Oh, he was so blasted clever! He had played all his cards right. Rita tossed fitfully on the rumpled bed.

"My God" she thought, "I almost made love to a man who wanted not my body, not my love only my death. Nothing but my death! She started to tremble. "Mama, Papa. Oh, God forgive me," she began to sob uncontrollably. She pushed the blankets down and beat her fists on her breasts. She continued to cry for some time and finally when she could breathe normally again she wasn't the least surprised to find herself naked in the pale moonlight. She had ripped and plucked her nightgown into pieces. Her only thought was to rid herself of every touch, every caress, every kiss she had ever given to that murderous David Swan. Rita could not bear the memory of how she had eagerly, lovingly thrown herself at David that night at Villa San Giovanni. Did he, also, remember that night and was he laughing at his silly, stupid prey? She felt so dirty, so debased.

She had to get clean again. Yes, Rita, thought frantically. Clean. She stood quickly, almost falling to the floor. She hung onto the furniture and made her way to the bathroom. Once inside the shower, she scrubbed herself furiously. A few deep bruises were still visible on her ribs, arms and legs although painfull to the touch, she scrubbed them roughly. Her shapely legs were back to normal size, the swelling having subsided. Her ribs only hurt when she moved a certain way. She reached up to shampoo her short, matted hair and cried out at the sharp pain that stabbed sharply in her side. Gritting her teeth she finished her shampoo and stepping from the shower, roughly towel-dried her sore body. She grabbed a toothbrush, she didn't care whose it was, brushed her teeth until the gums bled. Then rubbed her lips with hot soapy water. She rinsed and rinsed her mouth. Washing the ugly killer kisses down the drain. The face in the mirror stared back at her with strange haunted eyes. She wrapped herself in a large towel and started back to the rumpled bed. She paused at the large french-doors leading to the spacious balcony outside the darkened bedroom.

Below her she could see several men patrolling the grounds. They all carried rifles. As she stepped out on the balcony, two of the men looked up. Rita stood there shamelessly, wrapped in the bath towel. The moonlight gleamed on her golden hair, her naked ivory shoulders, her long slender legs. The two men nervously signaled a third man to join them. When this man looked up and saw Rita he waved, motioning her back into her room. But she stood strangely still. The man carrying his rifle close to his chest ventured closer and in a loud whisper pleaded with Rita.

"Miss Bond, please. It is best if you remain inside."

Rita knew he was right but in her confused mind she just couldn't go back to that bed. She was afraid. Afraid David would come in her dreams to kiss her, caress her with his bloody hands. She felt it would be easier to just throw herself over the balcony railing. She stepped outwards to grasp the cool, iron railing in her feverish hands.

"Miss Bond, please!" the rifleman whispered desperately as he dropped his gun to the ground, stepping directly under her. Suddenly, the lights in the next room flashed on. Spilling a soft shaft of yellow onto the balcony. The white drapes billowed softly in the open french-doors. Rita turned towards this new distraction. She walked slowly into the next room. The man below sighed in relief and snatched up his rifle, shaking his head he turned back to the other waiting men.

The room Rita had entered was long and spacious with a big, ornately carved desk dominating one end, while a huge bed filled the other end. Still hugging the bath-towel to her naked body, Rita padded over to the desk. It was covered with folders and legal drafts. Three huge law books stood between two brass eagles. Rita ran her hand over the leather bindings. Carlo. This is his room. She turned as he stepped from the bathroom clad in only pajama bottoms. His massive chest gleamed with tiny drops of water caught in the tight curly, black hair that all but covered his upper torso. He stood frozen.

"Margarita…"

Before he could move she ran across to him and threw her arms around his damp neck. Her towel slid down exposing her full, firm breasts which she pressed against his warm bare chest. She kissed him full on the mouth.

"Oh, Carlo, please love me."

"I do love you, darling." His arms came around her, pulling her tighter against him. She could feel the heat from his big hands on her naked back. His dark eyes searched her face then traveled down her slender throat to her full, bare breast. "Margarita," he whispered as he kissed her neck, then her soft firm breasts. Rita sighed as his lips brushed her harden pink nipples. He lifted his head and kissed her passionately on the lips. Pushing and probing with his hot insistent tongue.

"God, I've waited so long for you," he whispered huskily into her still damp, soft clean hair. Sweeping her up, he laid her gently on his huge bed. He flung the towel to the floor and she lay naked before his admiring gaze.

"You're beautiful. Absolutely beautiful," his hands caressed her nude body and Rita moved hungrily under his warm touch. She reached up, pulling him down on top of her. Their lips met. Their hot seeking tongues entwined over and around each other. Rita ran her hands over his broad back, down his strong, muscular arms, across his tapered waist, his slim hips, his firm hard buttocks. She felt him pressing against her. Huge and hard.

"Now," she thought feverishly. "Now, I'll wipe away forever the ugly memory of the murderous David. I never could have loved him like this. I know I couldn't. Never. Never!" She became frantic, moving this way and that, wiggling her hot hips up against Carlo.

"Oh, Carlo, please. Now. Now. Now."

Carlo grasped her shoulders and pushed her from him. He looked at her delirious eyes, felt her frenzied hands clawing at his back. "Margarita, what is it? What's wrong, darling?"

"Don't stop, Carlo. Don't stop," she kissed him again, hard on the mouth.

"I won't, darling. I don't ever want to stop." Carlo lay alongside her now, his hands caressing her hips, sliding between her hot thighs to caress her burning mound.

"Oh, yes, Carlo. Yes wipe it away. Push it out of my mind forever." She raised her hips into his hot probing hand. She was racing feverishly out of control. She just had to cleanse herself. She couldn't bear to ever remember David's touch. She had to burn him out. Forever.

"He never touched me there," she laughed. "I never did this with him. Never. Never!" she kissed Carlo's neck and wide shoulders while pressing more and more frantically into his hot, caressing hand.

Carlo's caressing slowed became less demanding. Gently, he

brought his hands up to cup Rita's warm face. She was smiling foolishly at him.

"I would have known," she said triumphantly "I would have known! Before we ever got this far. I would have known that he murdered my parents. And Bob! I'm sure I would have sensed something wrong. I would have known!" her eyes desperately sought Carlo's agreement.

"Of course, darling," he kissed her gently. "You would have known Margarita, because I would have told you. The first day he showed up at the Villa San Giovanni my instincts went haywire. I knew it was more than just plain jealousy.... because I had been insanely jealous of your fiancée, Bob. But what I felt towards David Swan was a much more intense suspicion." Rita cringed at the sound of David's name.

"No, Margarita, sweetheart. I knew that very night who he really was. I would never have let him touch you again," his thumbs wiped the tears starting down her flushed cheeks.

"Oh, Carlo. I hurt so. I hurt so bad inside. Love me. Make love to me. Make the hurt go away," Rita pleaded between sobs.

"Shh, darling. You don't know what you're saying."

"But I do, Carlo. I need you!"

"It wouldn't solve anything, Margarita. And you might regret it in the morning. Might even hate me for it," he rolled off the bed and walked over to the balcony doors.

Rita stared at his naked, muscular body. Her mind reeled back to a similar night in Urbino. Fear crept into her, chilling her feverish naked body. 'He's going to leave me, again; Oh, please. Carlo, please don't leave me…not now!'

And as if in answer to her unspoken prayer, Carlo turned and came back to the bed. He towered over her for a brief second then reached to each side of her and deftly whipped the covers she was laying on top of, down to her feet and then up over her naked body. He slipped in beside her, cradling her in his strong arms, he kissed her softly and lovingly.

"Go to sleep, my sweet. There'll be plenty of time for love-making later," he pulled her closer and soon Rita could sense by his warm, even breath that he was fast asleep. Only then did she allow her self the same luxury, for she had been terrified that he would suddenly arise and leave her alone with her haunting nightmares. Slowly she drifted into a warm, wonderous, dream free sleep.

Rita awoke to find herself still cradled in Carlo's strong arms.

"Good morning, darling," he kissed the tip of her nose.

She moved slightly and discovered that Carlo was indeed wide awake. Shocked at her own nakedness and conscious of the warm, hardness pressing on her naked thigh, she gave a small gasp.

"Yes, I think it's time I hit the showers," Carlo chuckled at Rita's frightened look "besides, you seductress, my arm is painfully numb."

"Oh, Carlo," Rita sat up quickly to free his arm, exposing her breasts in the process.

"You're even more beautiful in the daylight," he feasted his hungry eyes on her naked breasts.

She snatched at the bed covers, pulling them up to her chin. She glared at Carlo.

"Wonderful, wonderful," Carlo threw back his head gleefully. He grabbed her by the bare shoulders, pulling her up to him and then kissing her soundly. "You're your old self again."

"What old self? What are you talking about?" Rita blushed. She vaguely remembered the evening before. She wasn't quite sure what had happened. . .but she was grateful to Carlo for staying with her the whole, long, dark night. Although, right now, looking at his dark, lustfull eyes, she wanted to flee back to her own safe bedroom.

"I love you, Margarita," Carlo said solemnly, then roughly thrust her away and bounded angrily into the shower. Rita sat back on her heels, the covers still tucked under her chin, staring wonderously at the closed bathroom door. The steady, forceful beat of the shower, turned on full blast, snapped her out of her happy trance. She leaped from the bed and ran naked out along the balcony to her own room.

Rita's appearance at breakfast sent the two old Aunts into flutter of activity. They fussed over her, plying her with eggs, waffles, thick slices of sweet ham, fresh, crusty rolls and several mugs of hot, steaming coffee. Rita realized she was famished and happily accepted much more than she normally ate in the morning. As she was finishing her third cup of coffee, Carlo strolled in. He was dressed in a somber gray three-piece suit, white buttoned-down shirt and dark tie. In answer to her startled look he explained.

"I must fly down to Los Angeles. There's some legal business I have to attend to and there's an old friend I want to see. His name's Tom Malone. He's with the C.I.A," and with that turned his attention to a good-size steak and several eggs all but buried under a heap of hash-browned potatoes.

"I want you to stay inside the house, preferably in the same room with someone else at all times," he gestured with his egg-filled fork towards the Aunts. They in turn nodded their thin birdlike heads at Rita. She watched him consume the huge breakfast in silence. His brusque business manner was a far cry from his warm, loving mood earlier this morning. She realized he was concerned for her safety but she wished for and actually needed just some small gesture of tenderness.

"Carlo, I'll do anything you say," she thought she could soften his mood by being agreeable to his wishes for her safety. She smiled radiantly at him. But he didn't return her smile. His dark eyes bore piercingly into her. His jaw clenched, a muscle at the corner of his tight mouth twitched. He carefully pressed a napkin to his colorless lips, holding her frozen with his blazing glare.

"I'll be back this evening," he stated coldy, then left them sitting there nervously twisting their cold coffee cups.

The day passed all too slowly for Rita. She learned she was in Northern California. The beautiful Napa Valley stretched all around the lavish estate Carlo's family maintained. They were the richest and oldest family in the lush grape growing valley. Their vineyards here and in Urbino combined to dominate the wine industry. The Molza label indicated purity and quality. The Molza wines had won many awards, both in America and Europe. As Rita strolled about the many rooms, accompanied by Aunt Andrea until her old legs tired, then by Aunt L.M., she learned a great deal about Carlo Molza and his family. Most of the wide spread corporate legal work was handled by Carlo, while Dante handled the production and bottling, leaving the old man, Enrico Molza to tend to his first love—the growing and cultivating of new strains of grape.

"Don Molza's clear, delicious mountain chablis first created in the rugged Urbino mountains is considered the finest in the world." Aunt Andrea stated proudly. "In fact, why don't we have some with our lunch. Come, Margarita, lets find Louisa-Maria and have a bite of lunch."

And so the long day passed for Rita. She flatly refused to take an afternoon siesta knowing with her worry over Carlo's absence she wouldn't sleep. Instead, she sat in the library reading while the two exhausted Aunts dozed in the big, soft wing chairs before the fireplace. Their frail, thin hands folded primly in their laps, clutching the ever present lace hankies.

The more Rita learned about the Molza family, the more she was stunned by their enormous wealth. They had put their wealth into many good causes. Her own job at the museum was funded by a branch of a Molza trust. The World Federated Funds, which clothed and fed millions of homeless children, the Associated Atheletics Group, the Molza National Bank, all were owned or financed by the Molza family. The list went on until her head ached and she just closed the book in awe.

She felt foolish. Remembering how superior she had acted in Urbino. She had assumed they were all old-fashioned, not too successful in today's modern world. Yes, hadn't she screamed that at Carlo once? What an utter fool she had been. Just because they lovingly maintained some of the family customs that held the family together, she had snickered and flaunted her new liberated views in Carlo's face. Oh, no not Rita Bond. She wanted no part of the past. She wanted to bury Margarita Bondone. Forget all about the past. The past was too brutal. Too painful. What a foolish, young girl I've been… she thought. For now she felt years older. Everything she had been through these past few months proved to her how wrong she had been. "The past will always be with us. We can not change it, we can only learn from it," her thoughts whirled around in her aching head until wearily, she put her head down on the table and drifted off to sleep.

The short nap in the library had lessened some of Rita's tensness. Now as she showered and dressed for dinner, the thought that Carlo would soon be here again sent shivers of delight throughout her body. She was so lucky to have him! To think that she almost lost him by trying so hard to escape the past. He was part of her past and she no longer had to be afraid. Carlo would.be here. Protecting her, loving her. She blushed at the thought of their sleeping together. She felt a rush of heat, picturing his hard muscular body pressed so close to her own naked one. She knew positively that the next time their bodies were naked beside each other that Carlo would not be stopped. She trembled at the thought. Quickly, she finished dressing and ran down to dinner.

Her acute disappointment at not finding Carlo with the others vanished after one glass of wine, at which time, Carlo walked into the room smiling his big lopsided grin. Rita threw herself into his arms, kissing him hungrily.

"I'm so glad you're back," she pressed close to him.

"Well, with a welcome home like this, I'll have to go away more often," he grinned at her.

"No, Carlo, don't even joke about going away. I can't bear the thought of another day without you!"

"Wonderful. Because I've brought you a present." he held out a small black box. Rita opened it with shaking fingers. Inside lay a three-carat diamond ring, sparking brilliantly against the red velvet.

"Let's get married tomorrow, Rita." Carlo watched her with dark, expectant eyes. He slipped the big ring on her left finger.

"Father Vincenzo will be back and he can perform the ceremony in our own Chapel," he was kissing her soft, blonde hair. And before Rita could give him her answer both Aunts hurried forward.

"But Carlo…. your parents. You wouldn't deny them the joy of being at your wedding?" Aunt Louisa-Maria fretted.

"All the Molza's have always been married at San Giovanni. You know that Carlo," Aunt Andrea scolded.

"Basta! Basta! Enough!" snapped back an angry Carlo. "This is different," he folded Rita in his strong arms. "I want her with me always. I can not risk anymore fiascoes like that last auto accident. She was supposed to be watched. Protected. Well, what happened?" he glared furiously at the two old ladies, who began to shake at the sound of his angry voice. He released Rita and put an arm around each Aunt.

"I'm sorry. Forgive me. I didn't mean to lose my temper. But you must understand that until David Swan is apprehended Rita is in grave danger. I love her. I've always loved her. And I have no intention of losing her now." He turned back towards the dining table and sat each one down gently. Turning back towards Rita he demanded.

"Tomorrow?" his look was possessive and urgent.

She couldn't speak, her throat and mouth were so dry. She reached for her wine glass and peering over the crystal goblet at his dark, longing, lustful eyes she could barely nod her head.

He smiled a wide, relieved grin, "Well, now how about this great-looking beef," picking up his fork, he attacked the platter of rare roast beef. The three women only picked at the delicious roast. Andrea kept spearing glazed carrots daintly on her fork and then taking what seemed like an eternity to swallow each one.

Louisa-Maria, watching her, felt even more frustrated. She, herself ate very little but managed several glasses of wine.

Rita wasn't sure why she was thrilled one minute and then apprehensive the next. She loved Carlo. She was sure of that now. She certainly wanted him physically. So, what was nagging at her? Why wasn't she overjoyed at the thought of her wedding tomorrow? The dinner was finished in gloomy silence. Carlo the only one who seemed to enjoy any of the fine food. Coffee and Amaretto served in the small sitting room turned out even more awkward. The silences becoming longer as each wrestled with their own thoughts. Finally, by mutual consent they all trooped up to their respective beds.

Carlo gave Rita a quick kiss on the forehead and turned abruptly into his own room, slamming the massive oak door.

Later, laying on her own wide bed, Rita wondered about Carlo's quick Good-night. Probably, all for the best. She had a strong desire for him and she was sure he sensed her feelings. Her thoughts turned to her impending wedding. What on earth shall I wear? I haven't any clothes here. Will I even have the time to go out and buy a wedding dress? She fell asleep with visions of a lace-covered gown, a flower bedecked Church filled with friends floated through her dreams. Carlo's big muscular, half-naked body kept drifting closer and closer. She slept on, happy in her ecstasy unaware that in the next room her future husband tossed and turned, punching his sweat-drenched pillow with ill-contained fury.

Carlo, dark circles under his dark, impatient eyes, paced the floor like a wild lion. Running his wide hands through his thick black hair he kept repeating "Are you sure? Are you sure?"

The four, husky, dark-suited men all nodded.

"Sure about what?" Rita asked as she entered the sunny breakfast room. The men all stood, smiling happily at her.

"It is over, Signorina," one of the heavy men stated joyously. They all grinned and nodded.

Rita looked expectantly at Carlo.

"David Swan is dead," he answered her questioning eyes. She slumped into a chair, hand over her mouth.

"Yes, he has conveniently blown himself and five other terrorists to kingdom come!" Carlo sat down and poured Rita a steaming cup of coffee. She turned to the heavy set man who had first spoken.

"Please, what happened?"

"The Red Brigands had attempted to kidnap Ambassador Lentworth but the Police had been tipped off and were waiting. Unfortunately for the Brigands, their van, which was loaded with explosives, went up like a bomb when the Police fired on them.

Identifications were made through dental charts and the usual procedures," he stated quickly.

Rita shakily replaced the coffee cup and raised her hands to cover her face. She sobbed in blessed relief. The men made a hasty retreat while Rita cried quietly. She expected Carlo to take her in his arms but when she looked up he was staring stonily at her.

"Isn't it wonderful, Carlo. We're free now. Free, from that awful curse."

"Yes, dear, it's wonderful," he patted her arm solicitously.

Rita looked at him puzzled. She had expected mere of a reaction from him at this good news. But he sat strangely unmoved.

"Margarita, Carlo, how marvelous," Louisa-Maria glided into the breakfast room followed by Andrea both beaming radiantly.

"We just heard the news," they kissed and hugged Rita, then Carlo.

Sitting down they began to chatter both at once. Catching themselves they stopped. "You first, Andrea. You're the oldest," snapped Louisa-Maria.

Andrea threw her a quick, furious glance then turned to Rita. "Well, Margarita, now there's no reason to rush your wedding, we can all return to Urbino and have a nice proper wedding in San Giovanni Church." She cast a cautious side-long glance at Carlo, who sat stiffly at the head of the table.

"That's where your parents were married, dear," added Louisa-Maria smiling sweetly at Rita. Then turning to Carlo "And yours, also, Carlo Molza. The very idea! Marrying in a simple chapel!" she shook her bird-like head disgustedly. "We must fly back to Urbino as soon as possible. There is so much to do." The three women exchanged nervous looks.

"Yes, I'll make the arrangements," Carlo rose, throwing his napkin down, he quickly left the three women sitting in shocked silence. Rita had expected Carlo to resist any attempts to postpone the wedding. What was the matter with him? Was he now having second thoughts. Now that she was no longer in any danger maybe she didn't appeal to him. Was it just the thrill of danger he desired and not really her? She hardly heard the Aunts as they happily planned her wedding. She sat with a torrent of emotions boiling inside her. She finally excused herself. It was a bright, sunny day and she hadn't been outside for days. She slipped out into the lovely gardens surrounding the rambling brick house. The Molza's had several fountains scattered throughout the vast expanse of gardens. To Rita's surprise and delight she came upon a smaller version of the Tortoise fountain. This one made from a soft pinkish marble was more delicate than the fountain at Villa Sera. She sat on one of the benches, admiring the wide beds of red dahlias, blue and orange astees, and bright yellow and white chrysanthemums still blooming in the late November sun.

"Hello, Rita," a hoarse voice whispered from behind her. She whirled around, the scream dying in her frozen throat, as David Swan, one hand covering her mouth, dragged her into the shadows of the trees. He held a sharp, stiletto knife at her throat.

"I'm kind of glad you didn't die in the automobile accident. I have had a grand time planning what I was going to do when I found you again," he slashed her dress opening the bodice down to her navel.

She struggled silently in his iron grip. Jerking her head from side to side, desperate to let out even one small scream.

"Stop it, you bitch," he ran the knife point around her exposed nipple and Rita felt warm blood trickle down her breast onto her stomach. She froze. Too frightened to move a hair.

"That's better," he pushed her against a large willow tree. The long hanging branches hiding them from the path.

"Much better," David leered down at her terrified face. He pressed his cold lips hard against her trembling ones. Bile rose sour in her throat. She could feel the sharp knife pressing along her neck, down onto her other breast, circling the nipple but not penetrating the skin yet.

"Give me some tongue, baby," he whispered "Like you do for that Molza. Come on, Rita, be a good girl or I'll have to do some cutting."

Rita remained frozen. Her mind paralyzed by the touch of the icy knife point on her exposed breast. She stood with her eyes and mouth clenched tight.

"Now, Rita!" he pressed his cold lips on hers again, forcing his tongue between her clenched lips. Still she refused to respond.

"Stupid bitch!" he circled her nipple swiftly drawing blood this time. She gasped and clutched her hands to her bleeding breasts.

She glared at David. The pain sharpening her senses. She was sure David was completely out of control and would kill her any minute. He leered crazily at her. Spittle dribbling from the corners of his mouth.

"You know this is going to be much better than just killing you," he reached out with the knife slashing the lower half of her dress. Just then a large form crashed through the brush, snapping at David's arm. Breaking it like a small twig. The knife flew into the underbrush as he screamed out in pain. Carlo rage blazing from his dark eyes, then, shattered David's nose with a quick furious blow to the face. Another heavy punch threw the stunned David to the ground.

"Get up you filthy scum. Get up!" Carlo bellowed in rage. Anger and fury distorting his handsome face. But David lay broken and bloodied, a pitiful heap on the ground. Carlo turned to Rita, quickly stripping off his jacket, he covered her bleeding breasts.

"Oh, Rita, I'm sorry. I'm so sorry I didn't get here sooner," he kissed her tear-streaked face. He placed his hand gently on her bloody breast. "Damn, what did the bastard do?"

"It's just scratches, that's all," she tried to sound brave but her weak voice betrayed her terror.

"Come, darling. Let me get you inside," he swept her up in his arms. Just as a shot rang out…. whizzing right over Carlo's left shoulder. Ahead, they saw one of Carlo's men sighting down his rifle. Carlo whirled around in time to see David Swan on his knees with a pistol in his hand fall forward with a bullet hole between his icy blue eyes. The rifleman ran up beside Carlo, making the sign of the cross on his sweating brow. The three of them stared down at the dead David Swan.

"He was going to shoot you in the back," the rifleman said in complete disgust.

Rita sobbed and buried her head in Carlo's shoulder, weeping quietly.

"Gracie," Carlo and the rifleman exchanged a solemn look. Then with one last glance at the crumpled body on the ground, Carlo lifted Rita in his strong arms and hurried up to the house.

Later after washing the blood off her breasts, downing a couple of aspirins for her throbbing head Rita joined Carlo and the two Aunts on the sunny patio off the library. Carlo said, "I knew David Swan was not killed in that explosion. It was not his style to participate in any terrorists attacks. No, he had only one aim in life and that was to destroy the Bondone family. He was using those young terrorists to do his dirty work. He convinced them to set the stage for your parent's boating accident and your fiancée's car accident. He paid them well and also set up your cousin Paul's meeting with the gal whose brother was a member of the Red Brigands. It all led to a profitable arrangement for all of them. Paul's estrangement with the family and his lack of money turned his bitterness into something ripe for revenge. The Cignos wanted those jewels back. They believed their family was the rightful owners but your parents thought otherwise. Anna Taranta paid a terrible price for following her heart. She saw her first born child murdered and vowed the jewels would never be seen again. The broken hearted lovers hid the jewels somewhere on the grounds of Villa Sera and after extracting their bitter revenge on the Cigno and Taranta families they went on to have seven more children. My father and I are direct descendants of the old Don Molza who became very successful in real estate and finance. When Don Molza built the larger Villa San Giovanni he deeded Villa Sera to his loyal best friends the Bondone family.

After your parents inherited the Villa Sera your Dad surprised an intruder in the garden. They fought and in the struggle the intruder fell against the Tortoise on the fountain cracking his head open and dislodging the tortoise. Your father had no idea it was the long lost past coming back to haunt his family. It was an accident Rita," Carlo paused staring at Rita intently "When you ran down to the fountain and saw your Dad bending over Cigno he was trying to help him Rita. But stepping into that pool of blood and seeing it all over your shoes just freaked you out and your ran screaming back up the path where I grabbed you and tried to calm you but you were in shock, trembling and speechless. It was a terrible night for all and especially for a little girl. I have never forgotten it."

"Oh, so much blood. Much too much for two young children." Andrea wrung her hands her anxious eyes catching her sister Louisa-Maria's stony look across the room.

"That is the past. It is over. Over and done with. We have a new beginning with these two young people. They will start a new family without any of this ancient history hanging over them," Louisa-Maria stated firmly. While the very mention of starting a family with Carlo caused Rita to blush and cast a quick glance at him turning to face Sofia standing in the doorway.

"Senor Carlo. A phone call for you. A Miss Paige Donavan" she announced with a sharp glare at the two Aunts.

"Oh dear, oh dear," Andrea buried her face in her trembling hands.

"Hush you old fool," Louisa scolded her while watching Carlo. He had a frozen, startled look as if he just remembered something. Something very important. He hurried out to the phone without a word to anyone.

"What? What is it? Who is Paige Donavan?" Rita turned to the two sisters.

"Well we sort of forgot her in all the excitement. It certainly was not intentional was it Andrea?" responded Louisa.

"Oh, dear. No. No. I'm sure Carlo would have explained— will explain. Yes I'm quite sure," Andrea was white and trembling. "You see Paige is a lovely young woman. Truly a lovely young woman. She and Carlo—" she stuttered.

"Well, they were, oh dear, Louisa you must tell her. I just can not," Andrea threw her hands in the air pleading with her sister.

"Engaged," snapped Louisa looking directly at Rita. Who stood frozen thinking her heart must have shattered into a million pieces. What a fool I have been she thought. It was all a big sham. Her trust and love for Carlo was nothing but pure physical attraction. All those whispered lies. Nothing but lies. How could she have been such a fool. Without waiting for any more lies from Carlo she fled the library. Up to her room for her purse, back down the stairs to grab a set of keys from the foyer table. She could hear Carlo in the next room still on the phone with his fiancée the lovely Paige Donavan. Well good luck to that poor girl. Let her believe all his rotten lies. She was out of here. Outside she hurriedly started a gray SUV and drove quickly down the long driveway. She wanted to get as far away from the Molza vineyard and out of Napa Valley. She was so furious at her two Aunts. How could they have aided Carlo in keeping his dirty little secret. Oh, she really felt like a stupid fool. She couldn't wait to get back to her little Condo and her job. Hopefully one she still had. This whole experience was something she wanted to bury forever. She hated Carlo. Hated that lovely young woman Paige Donavan. Tears began streaming down her face obscuring her vision so badly that she had to pull over into a rest stop. That bastard Carlo!! All that talk about marriage and he was already engaged to another woman. Oh, how could he. Why did he do this? And those two old bats sitting there babbling about a wedding. Damn, damn. She pounded on the steering wheel. This is it. Absolutely no more Italy, no more so-called family for her. Wiping her eyes with a Kleenex she started the engine again pulling back onto the highway. Speeding out of the Napa Valley Rita was determined to forget Carlo Molza and start afresh back in Connecticut. She had no inkling of the furies in her future only concentrating on the speed it took to get away.

She left the SUV at a Park & Fly lot at the airport. Wrote a terse note to Carlo "Don't bother to call. I never want to speak to you again." She didn't bother to sign her name. The pain was bad enough writing Carlo's name on the folded note. She was lucky to get a Delta flight to Boston leaving in thirty minutes. With no luggage to check she made the gate just in time for boarding. As soon as the plane lifted into the night she fell wearily into a troubled sleep. The old dreams swirling around in her exhausted mind.

Upon landing, Rita grabbed a cab to the North End and retrieved her car and T-Bird. Heading straight for Connecticut while T-Bird squawked his displeasure at having been left behind. "Oh, please shut up, T-Bird. Please. I simply can not take any of your squawking tonight." Sensing her agitated mood the big bird flapped his wings indignantly then settled down quietly, watching Rita as she drove.

Four long hours later Rita finally arrived at her condo. Physically exhausted and emotionally weary. Even with a hot shower and a hot cup of Chamomile tea she was still wired and restless. Her body ached for Carlo's warm touch, her lips burned for his kiss but her mind could not forget his two-timing, sneaky, rotten actions. What kind of man was he? Kissing her, caressing her. Making her think she had finally found true love. And all the time he was engaged to another woman. Oh, the deceiving bastard. She dumped the teacup in the sink. Flicked on the kitchen light and stomped off to bed. It seemed only minutes before she was awaked by loud banging on the door.

"Open up, Rita," Carlo's angry voice bellowed. Afraid he

would disturb all the neighbors Rita quickly threw on a robe and opened the door.

"Are you crazy? What are you doing here? Didn't you read my note? Can't you understand?"

Carlo brushed by her slamming the door. "What the hell are you doing? Running away like this. You are not running away again Margarita." Carlo grabbed her by the shoulders, holding her away from him and pinning her with his blazing dark eyes. "All those years were Hell. Hearing about you second hand from the family. Praying you would speak again. Knowing I could have helped you. But everyone thought it best I keep away. No reminding you of that bloody night. You were too fragile. Well no more, Margarita. I am here, back in your life so get use to it," he kissed her firmly, then released her and walked over to the sofa and collapsed in a tired heap.

"Carlo, why are you doing this? I know you are engaged to a lovely young woman, Paige Donavan, the Aunts told me about her. Please don't torture me any longer. I can't bear it," she slumped on the sofa.

"Bastard. Mean lying bastard!" T-Bird sounded really mean as he observed the two sitting on the sofa.

Carlo was startled by the sound of another voice. "Well, well the famous T-Bird. Hello there buddy," he nodded at the big parrot sitting on the top of the bookcase.

The big grey studied Carlo intently for a minute. "Yes, famous.

Very famous. And Hello to you too," then flew across the room to the top of the drapery rod. The sharp eyes staying on Carlo.

"Remember when I had to leave Urbino and return to California? I wanted to tell Paige in person that our engagement was off, that I had fallen in love with you. But she had flown to Paris and was touring Europe with friends. I was unable to reach her and was anxious to get back to Urbino and you. I was worried about you alone in Urbino. Well, not exactly alone but without me. I lost you once and I didn't want to go through that again. Rita, I love you and want to marry you," he took her in his arms, pressing his face into her blonde curls breathing in her soft scent. "No more running away, please, darling."

Rita felt all her fears melting away. Replaced by a sense of finally belonging. Of finally being back where she really was meant to be. "Yes, Carlo, yes. No more running."

"No running. No more running," T-Bird flew over their heads to his cage. And they barely heard him as they kissed.

CPSIA information can be obtained at www.ICGtesting.com
Printed in the USA
BVOW05s1211250416

445497BV00001B/50/P